WORLDS BETWEEN

a River of Lakes novel

CARL NORDGREN

This is an uncorrected proof and text may change before final publication. Please verify with author or publisher before quoting directly from this text.

Worlds Between
Carl Nordgren
cnordgren.lightmessages.com
cnordgren@lightmessages.com

Published 2015, by Light Messages
www.lightmessages.com
Durham, NC 27713

Paperback ISBN: 978-1-61153-134-3
Ebook ISBN: 978-1-61153-133-6

To Marie, my wife, always.

To Steve Fobister and Robin Metz,
two great men who have been my guides whether near or far.

Chapter 1

A CHILD IS BORN

THIS MAN STOOD ON THE ALERT outside the door of the large wigwam, his flintlock primed and at the ready; he had tied a sprig of cedar together with a hawk feather near the muzzle of the barrel of his gun. The people of the village and their visitors were gathering around the wigwam and two of the men carried rifles; Brian Burke had his recently purchased Marlin 336 and Albert Loon carried the old Winchester that had been in his clan for as long as he could remember; both rifles were lever-action, both 30-30s.

From inside the wigwam a woman's hard moans and deep groans suddenly became sharp cries. The cries grew and grew into calls of the purest pain that lasted, the men thought, much too long, until a sharp bark of agony was followed by a moment of silence, inside the wigwam and outside, and then by the baby's first wail, greeted by the joyous relief of many voices, from inside the wigwam and then outside.

Brian watched for Albert's indication to fire their rifles as he listened for news from inside and hoped to hear his invitation to enter.

Inside the wigwam Maureen received her new born baby from the Nokomis who had received it from the Ojibway midwife who had attended Maureen throughout the later stages of her pregnancy and presided over the delivery, observed by the nurse from the hospital in Kenora that Brian insisted at least be present.

Mary Fobister, Maureen's closest friend, was the other woman attending; she had supported Maureen, propping and balancing her, holding her up, stroking her and comforting her, during what became a furiously fast delivery.

From inside Maureen called out to her husband, "Brian, it's —" just as This Man raised his gun to his shoulder and aimed high above the trees out over the River, the talisman at the tip of his gun twirling its magic in the breeze, and Brian and Albert raised their rifles together, so that in the same moment Maureen's voice called she was greeted by the thunder of the rifles proclaiming a child is born.

Brian exchanged handshakes with his closest friends and everyone stepped forward to touch him and offer blessings, and Maureen was calling him in as the nurse from Kenora emerged from the wigwam door with a sweet smile of wonder on her face and assurance in her voice; Brian handed his rifle to Albert and knelt to enter.

Maureen looked up at him, exhausted, her hair sweated to her face, and gave her husband a smile; Mary moved back to make way for Brian who crouched in next to his wife and baby. Maureen whispered, "Grace O'Malley Burke has come to live with us."

He patted his wife's shoulder, studying her status, then touched the little one's shoulder with his finger. "You knew. You were right."

"I never doubted."

"That sound she made. It was grand, yeah."

"You should have felt her fightin' her way out into the world."

Brian looked around at the interior of the wigwam and shook his head.

"An' you were right about all of this as well."

"I was glad you brought the nurse in. It was comfortin' to see her there."

"But you didn't need her."

"We didn't need her."

"All because you wanted our daughter to be born in a wigwam."

"No, because I wanted our daughter to be born with her people gathered 'round."

Chapter 2

GUESTS AND VISITORS

THE GREAT LODGE HALL at Innish Cove—the grand building Brian had dreamed of and Maureen had planned for from the beginning—took most of two years to build and was completed the same year their daughter Grace O'Malley Burke was born, in 1953. Maureen supervised the construction well into her pregnancy, and only in the final days did she leave it to Brian to oversee the work on the massive log structure that captured under one vaulted roof a full dining hall, a great rock fireplace and its sitting area, a pub corner with bar and a billiards table and lounge, and a spacious kitchen with two stoves and two ovens, three sinks deep and wide, and a walk-in pantry big enough for flour barrels and plenty more.

Three weeks after Grace O'Malley was born, Brian and Albert Loon and the younger men and boys of Joe Loon's clan took the tables and chairs and the two-way radio and kitchen supplies out of the cabin that from the first days of operation had served the camp as the guests' dining hall and moved them into the Great Lodge—the first few tables that had crowded the cabin seemed lost in the dining room's full expanse—and the guests were served supper there for the first time the middle of that summer. Brian and Maureen held their baby daughter between them as they entertained their guests with stories of the founding of Innish Cove.

The fifth summer following that first meal in the Great Lodge's dining hall, as the evening brought a delightful cool to the blazing hot mid-August day, Brian and Maureen stood together in the pub visiting with guests after supper. During his trip back to Ireland to visit his children—Tommy and Katie were present to him; Patrick continued to keep what he thought of as a safe distance—Brian collected Guinness signs and posters, including the poster of a Toucan balancing a pint on his beak under the headline "Lovely Day for a Guinness."

This sign was centered behind the bar and over a shelf of bottles, one each of every sort of Irish whiskey, and not just Bushmills and Jameson, but Inishowen and Black Bush, Redbreast and Greenore, and Tullamore Dew, and nearly a dozen others Brian also collected on the trip. He found that whether the guests drank the Irish or simply toasted them, they all enjoyed the look of the labels.

The pub opened out onto the Great Hall's dining room now close to crowded with tables where some guests who had stayed out on the River's lakes until late were just mid-meal, while others were finishing their steaks and baked potatoes and some sat back to sip an after-supper coffee, freshly brewed. Guests at two separate tables began the first rounds of four-handed gin games there in the Great Hall before they would retire to their cabins with their cards and their drinks and stories of the day's adventures fishing the River, and its lakes with the best of friends, guided by real life Indians.

The supper tables were cleared and cleaned by two teenage Ojibway girls, dressed in white blouses and black skirts that Mary Fobister selected and Maureen approved, each using red ribbons to tie back their shiny black hair. It only took one guest to engage the girls enough to get past the reserved quiet and natural shyness the girls maintained around guests, and then finally work out that the girls weren't sisters as most guessed but cousins, the tall one Ruthie Strong, the younger girl Sweet Marie, and the collected information was then passed on over the summer from guest to guest as the arcs of trips overlapped.

The Great Lodge was covered by a vaulted ceiling, and its log walls were nearly fourteen feet high. Even so the walls were covered with the visual evidence of successful trips and delighted guests. Moose heads were the largest and hung highest; black bear heads were most dramatic, with their toothy snarls. Trophy mounts of northern pike, walleye, smallmouth bass, lake trout, Canadian geese, and the antlered heads of white tail deer were most plentiful. Small bits of brass tacked to the trophies' wooden frames noted the hunters or fishermen and the dates of their glorious adventures.

Placed among them were photographs, mostly black and white, of guests with this trophy or that one, some photos a series that captured seasoned regulars, some with guides included, a couple of guests quite renowned, others near famous.

Maureen was the first to retire from the work of entertaining guests in the evening, though she would stay as long as any female guests were in the Great Lodge. That wasn't often. The guests were men, successful men, men traveling with their fishing and hunting clubs, men and their young sons, men and their old sons, men with their business associates, and so it was this evening as Maureen attended to last details in the kitchen before she left for the night. When she determined all was ready for breakfast in the morning she returned to the Great Hall's lounge to locate young Grace O'Malley, expecting her to be sitting with guests while they told her their stories and she told them hers. She remembered the last place she'd seen her daughter playing and she spied her there still.

Grace O'Malley was asleep, in the arms of one of their guests. The little girl's raven black hair spilled across the guest's grey and white beard. Earlier in the evening Maureen had checked with the guest to make sure her daughter's play wasn't tiring him out; he had winked back at Maureen over his toothy grin and told her to go away. They had been playing some sort of hidden ball game then, but now she was held safe in Ernest Hemingway's arms, lying on his chest, as he sat back in a big overstuffed chair by the fire. Hemingway's son, Patrick, and their two friends spoke softly so they wouldn't disturb the scene. The quiet corner setting had been Hemingway's all four nights he had been in camp. Maureen directed Brian's attention to the scene then said good night to the guests she passed at the billiards table on her way to Hemingway's corner.

He saw her coming, grinned again, and spoke softly now over the child's head.

"I love sleep. My life has a tendency to fall apart when I am awake, ya know."

Maureen smiled down at her daughter and Hemingway stroked the girl's curls as he looked up at Maureen.

"You've got a gift for naming things."

"Namin' things?"

"This place is surely the Great Lodge at Innish Cove. And I've heard the stories of Ireland's pirate queen who went nose to nose with Queen Elizabeth the First, the legendary Grace O'Malley."

"Outside our own, not many know of her. Brian's ancestors married O'Malleys."

"I can see this child of yours is a warrior one moment, a princess the next, and always of the most extraordinary sort."

"Well, she is a little thing, yeah, small for her age you see. She's five, an' I think folks are comparin' her to three year an' four year olds."

"I'm not comparing her to anyone or anything. I am just appreciating the powerful beauty radiating from all she does."

Maureen smiled. "Well, thanks. All of you, you've been so kind an' so patient with her, with your playin' an' all your attention."

"Child's play is its own reward. I was long ago a convert to it, child's play and the joy of joy. Seems I've forgotten it lately."

"You bring her joy. She'll miss you."

Maureen reached for Grace but Hemingway held her there. "Ah, but the weight of her feels good on my chest."

"See now I'm bein' selfish here for I can't settle into my own bed until I know this character's safely tucked into hers. Unless you want me sleepin' on your other shoulder, so…"

Hemingway lifted the child but Maureen knew she needed to do most of the work. She'd noticed time and again as he made his way around the camp and in and out of boats that the pain he lived with had weakened him. She bent quickly to collect Grace O'Malley into her arms, held her close with the girl's head resting on her shoulder, and addressed the guests with her smile.

"Your plane's here half-eight. Just leave luggage at the cabin door when you come up for breakfast an' we'll be by to collect it."

Patrick Hemingway's appearance was a near perfect replica of his father's at the same age. He asked Maureen. "A favor our last night?"

"Of course."

"Ask your husband for a moment of his time, if he has a moment—I see the guests' demands on it. But we've just heard mention of your fight against the hydroelectric dam, and we'd like to hear the full story."

"His stories are always full, yeah."

The men laughed and Papa took over again.

"Let him know he has an interested audience. That's all a storyteller needs to hear."

Maureen turned and wove her way through the guests, nodding good night, then stopped to trade kisses with Brian and to let him plant one on his daughter's head as she shared the Hemingway request. She left through the kitchen, empty now, and headed out into the nighttime forest with its dark paths.

She took the path across the small sandy clearing that led to the grove of birch and the Chapel. There the path narrowed to one marked Private that climbed a gentle and heavily wooded slope to a house, their home, built on a broad flat step, a small plateau just high enough to look out over the fishing camp she and Brian, and Joe Loon's clan were still creating, still building.

Maureen began each day in the Chapel, usually with Brian, in quiet contemplation and prayer. Whenever she passed the Chapel during the day she would whisper the same brief prayer. And at the end of her day, as she headed home for the night, she always went in.

It was dark but she was practiced at balancing Grace, so she could strike a match and light two candles on the table at the head of the small room. There was a bench near the corner where the recent addition to the Chapel stood, a tall statue carved from a tree trunk.

The statue itself was four feet tall and sat on a foot-high section of tree trunk for a pedestal. Maureen pushed the bench with her foot so she could sit just where she liked, right in front of the statue and just below, the carved image of Joseph the father struggling to contain and support his laughing, scrambling baby boy, young Jesus, the toddler who had climbed out of his father's arms and up onto his shoulders in a joyous adventure to look down upon Maureen and her daughter.

The statue's painted surfaces were fresh and bright in the candlelight; the flame's flicker across the two carved faces turned their smiles to laughter; the statue's recesses were shadowed pure black and seemed unending. Brian had commissioned the statue from a Grassy Narrows wood carver three years after the Chapel was built and the work represented countless hours of careful craft.

She held her daughter close as she admired the skill, rough but complete. Maureen was still for quite a few minutes and then she prayed, ending with the same words every night, those words she prayed each time she passed, words she had to say aloud.

"An' may God bless the Innocents."

She crossed herself, left the candles burning—for others were more likely to stop in if a light beckoned—and she carried Grace O'Malley up the dark path to the house with its own inviting light in the window, one set by an Ojibway employed as a camp laborer sent by Brian.

❊ ❊ ❊

Brian brought a bottle of Black Bush and glasses for his guests and told the Hemingways and their friends the story of their string of failed legal battles against the construction of the Ontario Hydro dam on the eastern branch of the River, one that meandered along for some distance before merging back into its sister channel fifteen miles north for the River's long run and circuitous route on toward Hudson Bay. Brian explained the strategy behind the series of legal filings they made with a number of ministries, after Joe Loon and Albert told them that there was a small Ojibway burial site along with traditional trapping lines and wild rice flats that would be flooded by the dam, and he was interested in hearing what the writer might say about it; at the time Brian had been opposed to it, considered it wasted money, and tried to convince Maureen it was pointless.

"How far along were they in the construction?"

"Over two years, close to three, after years of plannin'. There was no way we would stop 'em."

"You had no intention of stopping them. You were sending a

message."

"That was Maureen's goal. What she said was that this fight was to set us in a better place to win the next one, yeah, whatever the next one might be, to make sure everyone understood that we're all in to protect the River, always. She likes to think three or four steps ahead like that, while I sweep up behind."

"And smile."

"*Mostly* I smile."

The others settled back in their chairs looking forward to the writer and the camp owner's conversation.

"Since they argued that this burial site should be dismissed because it was so small an' because it was abandoned, just four graves before the village was wiped out by smallpox a hundred years ago, then Maureen says we have them on record sayin' that size is a relevant legal distinction, an' if a site is still bein' used, that's a legal distinction, which leads to arguin' that larger active burial sites along the River should be respected an' protected."

"That's nice logic, but they won't respect it if they find it's to their advantage."

"Our attorney thinks it's got standin'."

"What do you figure as your reckoning?"

"Reckonin'?"

"When you take a principled position and claim a truth that no one wants to hear, there's always a reckoning. I've experienced it every time I've made the mistake of being principled."

His friends laughed; Patrick knew of the sadness behind that comment and barely smiled.

Brian offered the bottle again.

"We've lost friends. We hadn't many, in Kenora anyway, once our first fight was made known, against the pulp mill. Our produce supplier refused our business when Maureen made it clear we weren't goin' away easy, but that just led us to the Mennonites who keep us pretty well-stocked, an' of course NOA lost all our business from the mills, an' that was a good bit. Slowin' the dam a few months cost them a better part of the construction season an' that delayed a pulp mill bein' built a year an' that cost us maybe five thousand in lost revenue, so."

"So there's plenty of folks who don't like what you did."

"As much as it cost us, it cost them more, much more. Their story is we did it for selfish reasons an' they're right, God bless 'em, they're right. It's not good for my business to have civilization creepin' in too close. I sell wilderness adventures, an' if guests fly in over roads an' dams an' power lines an' paper mills, well, that'll change their view of what this place is about for them. But that doesn't mean I didn't do it for some very good reasons as well."

Papa had taken over the bottle and was refilling each glass and then he raised his.

"A toast to some very good reasons."

❋ ❋ ❋

The next morning the NOA Grumman Goose that would carry Hemingway and his friends out of camp and back to Kenora crested the far southeastern ridge on its way to The Great Lodge at Innish Cove. The plane's shadow skipped over the River's lakes. Brian and Maureen had recently added the Goose to the NOA fleet. The plane offered a touch of luxury, which in the wilderness simply meant more clean comfort. This plane sat six passengers very comfortably in cushioned chairs, not canvas benches, with a window for each row of seats.

Only two new guests, James Conaty and James Brislanne, were flying in to camp in the Goose that morning. Since they had taken off from Lake of the Woods and left Kenora behind, they were sitting across from each other, staring out fuselage windows, the view to the east looking like the view to the west; both of the Jameses were transfixed by the grand sweep of lakes, some of them part of the massive River system, many landlocked, often dotted with islands large and small, rocky and wooded, and by the fir forests and birch groves, and clusters of maple, and the marshes and streams and ponds, and low lying grey-blue granite ridges and rocky outcroppings, as far as the eye could see, nearly as much water as land, and only a couple of logging roads the last half of the trip.

The two Jameses were Chicagoans, South Side Irish, James Brislanne, a homebuilder, and James Conaty, a lawyer, both from Bridgeport.

And the two Jameses were of the small group of community

leaders who spearheaded the revival, over the past ten years or so, of the Chicago unit of Clan na Gael, organized to support the IRA in their fight against British occupation of Northern Ireland.

The fuselage windows offered no view ahead of the plane, so when the bush pilot called back that the Great Lodge just came into view, dead ahead, for the two Jameses it was all water and woods.

The homebuilder called out to the lawyer.

"She did one hell of a job picking her hiding place."

"Kevin calls her a master."

"But he found her."

They were quiet, though the homebuilder seemed anxious when he spoke up again.

"I hope I don't embarrass myself when I'm out in the boat, when we're fishing. The only fishing I've ever done was for perch, with my old man, on Lake Michigan, from the shore. I was just a boy. I don't remember I liked it much."

"You never liked doing anything with your old man."

"He was a mean son of a bitch… I've never even been in a boat."

"You've never been in a boat?"

"Not counting walking a ship that was tied up at Navy Pier."

The plane crossed the lake and flew a low circle over the cove so everyone in camp and especially any late-departing guides knew the pilot's intention, which was to claim priority for his landing on the broad expanse of the River's open lake, Rainbow Lake, just outside Innish Cove.

When the Goose passed overhead Simon Fobister and a second young Ojibway boy were carrying the Hemingway party's luggage to the dock, and Brian emerged from his office at the foot of the dock as the boys passed. They piled the suitcases and valises and tackle boxes and rod cases at the end of the dock, where Joe Loon and Albert were tending to their boats dockside, then left to get the guests' boxes of fish fillets from the ice house.

Joe Loon and Albert had been the Hemingways' guides. Now Albert was preparing his boat to take the two Jameses out after they settled in a bit from their travels; Joe Loon was preparing his boat for a full day trip with Simon and Brian, leaving as soon as the Goose departed.

Joe Loon often spoke to Albert about the big spirits of the white men who came to this place, and as he loaded the extra gas can from the dock to his boat he continued.

"When they leave for their journey home I can see the spirits of Big Brian's guests know they have been living at a sacred place. These white men who come here, they all have big spirits. Sometimes their big spirits have a sickness. Some have a very big sickness and haven't seen it yet. But they all listen to the spirits of this place. Even those whose sickness makes them deaf. There are many reasons Big Brian's Dream sent him here to build this camp at this sacred place. To help us protect the River. And to heal the white man's spirits."

"Joe Loon's Dream has shown its great powers. Everyone sees that."

When Brian walked up to stand with them, Albert translated what Joe Loon said next.

"Joe Loon asks about the white man called Him Way. Joe Loon wonders what it was that caused this great spirit to become broken."

"Africa. That's the name of a wilderness land far away from here. Hemingway was in a bush plane flyin' over that country on a huntin' trip, 'cept in Africa they don't have the River an' all the lakes you have here, it's just the land, yeah, just forests an' plains, they call it the bush like we do here, so their bush plane was rigged with wheels to land on the ground. Hemingway was a great hunter in Africa an' he flew over the bush country many times to get to the best huntin' grounds, but this day his plane had engine problems, an' when his pilot tried an emergency landin', well, they crashed into some trees. Hemingway was nearly killed. In fact the first stories told about the crash said he was killed."

Brian paused throughout for Albert to translate for Joe Loon, who replied at the end, "Some face death and leave it behind. Some face death and carry it with them."

"Well, the poor sod had to face it all again. Just when he was recoverin', another plane he was flyin' in crashed on take-off an' again he was nearly killed. The poor man; he was once so vigorous, but now his body is filled with pain."

"His great spirit is wearing away from this pain he carries. This is what Joe Loon sees."

❄ ❄ ❄

When the Goose passed over the camp, Maureen was in the kitchen with the cook and staff—one male chef, a recent Hungarian immigrant Maureen recruited from a fine restaurant in Toronto, and Ojibway women and girls, with Mary in charge of all but the cooking, and Maureen helping out during busy times, which was often these days. They cleaned up from breakfast, planned for supper, and checked on supplies. Maureen excused herself a moment, bent down under the work table set up in the least busy corner of the kitchen, and there she found Grace O'Malley playing with six-year-old Little Stevie, Mary's son and Joe Loon's grandson. Grace crawled out at her mother's call, took her mother's hand, and followed Maureen through the swinging double doors from the kitchen to the dining hall.

Most guests ate breakfast quickly to get out on the water for early walleye success, so the only table occupied was the Hemingway party, and they were getting up to go. Maureen's study of the old man's aches and pains told her he'd wince as he stood and limp as he turned, and he did, though he hid the evidence of his damage well.

"Grace O'Malley wanted to say good bye to Papa an' Uncle Patrick an' all her new friends."

"She isn't going to come down to the dock to see us off?"

"No, no. When there's planes about an' guests leavin' an' comin' an' supplies loadin' an' unloadin' that's too much commotion, so we keep her off dock."

Hemingway favored his side but still winced as he knelt down to the child.

"Well then, before I go, I have one last secret to tell my lovely Grace O'Malley. Can I whisper it in your ear?"

She nodded.

"Which ear for our secrets?"

She pulled back a sweep of her black curls—the raven black she shared with her mother that caused some new guests to wonder if Brian's wife and daughter weren't indigenous, or partly so—and she held them out of the way.

"This one."

"Okay, but first you must promise Papa you won't tell anyone."

13

"Yes Papa, I promise."

"Okay." The big bearded man leaned forward to tickle the little girl's ear with the whiskers on his chin and she giggled and danced away.

"It appears that ear's become too ticklish. I'll bet we've got too many secrets already dancing around in that one. What if we tried your other ear?"

Grace O'Malley spun on her toes to offer her other ear. Hemingway placed his lips just close enough and softly said, "I was reading a book one day and it said that Grace O'Malley was a beautifully brave girl. And a brave beautiful girl."

He turned back to her full face and said, "In truth, madam—"

Grace O'Malley folded her arms across her chest and stamped her foot and insisted "Mademoiselle!"

"Pardon me. Yes, of course, mademoiselle, but I do have one more secret."

She smiled, and she nodded her head yes as he returned to her ear.

"That book I was reading, it also said Grace O'Malley grew up to be a great woman."

Looking far away Grace O'Malley said, "That's me. Mum tells me lots of stories about Grace O'Malley and they end with me." She looked up at her mum. "I want another story about us tonight."

"We'll worry about tonight tonight. Now give Papa a big hug for he must be leavin' us to go back to his home."

They hugged and Grace held on as Hemingway tried to stand with her, but Maureen peeled her daughter away and held her in her arms.

"If you gentlemen'll head on down to the dock I'll meet up with you there."

She carried her daughter back into the kitchen where she found Mary. Mary returned Grace to the world she and Little Stevie had been building under the table—since early in the season the two children had been collecting pine cones and favorite River stones and a worn bit of deer antler, and a couple of wood carvings of graceful animals and small pieces of driftwood that came to the same graceful form naturally; they had arranged and rearranged these pieces to create fantasy worlds while their mothers worked together with the others above them.

Before she left, Maureen checked her schedule for the day against Mary's then headed down to the dock to join Brian to greet the new guests and say farewell to the departing. Hemingway and his party walked slowly down the path in deference to the pain in Hemingway's step, and Maureen caught them as they left the trees and walked along the top of the beach. She took the writer's arm and waved to Brian waiting for them on the dock.

✻ ✻ ✻

Outside the cove, on the lake identified as Rainbow Lake on maps but known to the Ojibway as Kaputowaganickok, the Lake where the Funereal Fires Burned, the last fishing boats had passed and guests enjoyed watching the spray from the Goose's belly landing splitting the surface of the lake.

The plane taxied towards the cove as Hemingway summoned strength for this performance and led his friends onto the dock, holding hands with Maureen now, and calling out to Brian.

"If Brian Burke isn't the goddamn luckiest fellow on the face of the earth I can't imagine the greater fortune. You wake each day in God's country with the most beautiful woman by your side…"

Hemingway released Maureen with a bit of a bow that caused a hurt and then stood respectfully in front of Joe Loon, who upon his guests' approach had climbed out of his boat so he too could offer mutual respect and stand with this man. Hemingway took Joe Loon by the shoulder.

"…And you have the honor of being in partnership with one of the last true humans our modern world will allow."

Joe Loon took the writer by the shoulder and said, "This man tells two stories. He is the only one who understands both of them."

"I love the sound of that too much to have anyone translate it for me."

Maureen found her way to Brian's side as she told Papa, "He calls you a great storyteller."

Brian added "My luck an' privilege is to share it all with folks who love it for it's true worth."

"We'll be back next year. We may try to get here earlier in the season and go after lake trout this time, maybe stay a full week."

Patrick was shaking Brian's hand. "I'm afraid I won't be able to make it; I don't come back over too often."

"Tanzania, that's a haul. I have a son named Patrick in Ireland an' he and I don't get to see each other often." Then Brian included all in his comments. "We know how busy a life you lead an' if you can find time for a return trip, we'd be delighted to have you."

Maureen offered, "Just send us the dates you'd like to come an' we'll hold them for you while you work it out, yeah."

"An' with your say so, Papa, that big pike you caught your first day out, I'll get it mounted an' put it over your photo in your corner."

"Marvelous. Give people something worthwhile to remember me by."

❋ ❋ ❋

James the homebuilder called James the lawyer to his window when he discovered that the plane's turn exposed the camp to his view.

"I see her. Black hair, the red shirt… the only woman on the dock. That's gotta be her."

The lawyer arrived at the window in time to see her turn to hug a big bearded man.

"The photo of her made her out to be pretty…"

As the Goose drew nearer, the woman in the red shirt tossed her black hair and laughed at something the man told her.

"…but she's, I mean she's…"

"Stunning."

The homebuilder hesitated.

"Yeah, stunning… And a little intimidating?"

"I was going to say exciting."

"Don't you get a little intimidated by exciting women? I do."

"Really? I get excited when women try to be intimidating."

"That fellow she's talking to, the old man with the beard. He look familiar to you?"

"I'm watching her."

❋ ❋ ❋

The Goose's glide carried it to the dock. Brian and Albert were well practiced at catching the wing to guide its float up and over the dock so the plane could be tied dockside.

As Brian stepped forward to unlatch the Goose's fuselage door to let the guests out, he turned to Hemingway.

"My famous guests honor us when they tell others about us, but now you're meetin' the sort who fills up our cabins, Chicago businessmen an' factory owners. They're the bread an' the butter."

Brian opened the door and the homebuilder stepped out just as he realized who the bearded man was. "Jesus, you're that Old Man and the Sea."

"That's the best exit line anyone's got a right to expect."

They laughed and shook hands all around. Ojibway boys removed luggage from the plane then loaded luggage, and Maureen gave both Hemingways final hugs. Before Albert and Brian pushed the Goose away from the dock Brian told the pilot to swing by the new dam so Papa and his friends could see it.

The Ojibway boys carried the two Jameses' luggage to their cabin. Watching the Goose taxi out of the cove, Brian and Albert began to plan the rest of the day for the guests, and Maureen wandered over to Joe Loon's boat.

Maureen had worked with Mary Fobister and two or three other Ojibway women nearly all day every day during the fishing season for a half a dozen years, and she had learned quite a bit of their language. Mary enjoyed teaching her, and Maureen loved speaking with Joe Loon.

"The River and its banks behind the dam will be flooded."

"My Grandfather trapped there with his father."

"That is the Place where the People Trap the Biggest Beaver?"

"Yes. North on the River where the white man dug their mines to take the gold, that is the Place where Moose Grows the Largest Antlers. I am taking Big Brian to find what has happened to the Biggest Beaver. It is a hard trap line to cover, and one best for the young men, but it is there the beaver have pelts as big as two big males. It was good for mink along the shore when I was a boy but they are gone. The Biggest Beaver have always been there."

"Will they just move up the side of the valley as the water rises?"

"I will look for signs. They might have moved up the side of the valley. But they might have gone up the River."

"You are not angry about the dam."

"The young men on the reserve can be angry because they are not searching for the truth of what is happening."

They watched the Goose take off, then Maureen led the guests to their cabin and Brian waited with Joe Loon for Simon's return. Simon jogged back to the dock, passing Maureen along the top of the beach. He stopped at the storage shed at the foot of the dock, grabbed a knapsack he'd stuffed with food and drinks, trotted down the dock's length, and settled into the bow seat of Joe Loon's boat. Joe Loon cranked the engine, Brian pushed off from the dock, and they motored across the cove out into Rainbow Lake as the Grumman Goose disappeared across the far ridge, headed southeast.

A fresh wind was just stirring up a light chop on the open water of the River's lake as Joe Loon steered the boat in the same direction the Goose was flying.

❈ ❈ ❈

The two Jameses sat in their cabin, assembling fishing tackle. The homebuilder was threading the line through the rod ferrules.

"So we agreed how we'd start?"

"Did we?"

"I think so."

"Jigging for walleyes?"

"I bought a bunch of the same sort of yellow jigs our Indian was recommending."

"Our guide. Not our Indian."

"Pretty cool, don't you think. Having an Indian guide."

"Definitely....Let me see your jigs… I think I bought some like that except a size or two bigger."

Their rods assembled, the reels mounted, line threaded, they tied on metal leaders as Brian had instructed. They'd changed from travel clothes to fishing clothes and were ready to leave the cabin to meet Albert at the dock, when the lawyer decided it was time to review the situation.

"With Burke gone for the day I'm thinking we should deliver the package to her right now."

"If Kevin's right and she's still not told Brian of her IRA ties, then maybe we're better off talking to her when he's in camp. If she's gonna get angry that we're here, his presence keeps her under control."

"I think we act now. The sooner we give her the package the more chances we have to talk it over with her during our trip. Kevin gave us plenty of angles for convincing her... She said she was headed to the Lodge if we needed her for anything."

"Then let's go."

The lawyer removed a large sealed envelope from his suitcase, folded it, and stuck it in his back pocket. The two Jameses stepped out of the cabin with their tackle boxes and fishing rods in hand but headed up the path that led to the Great Lodge.

❄ ❄ ❄

Ernest Hemingway sat in the co-pilot's chair. The pilot pointed out the first glimpse of the dam on the horizon, at one o'clock. Power lines ran south and vanished at the horizon.

"Those power lines head where the pulp mills have been expanding. I'm sure Brian told you about how he and Maureen tried to stop it."

"They slowed it down. When the other side has all the money and all the political power, that's no small accomplishment. "

"All they really did was cost some folks a lot of money and make a whole lot of other people angry at them."

Behind the dam the wide River forest valley was now flooded by a long narrow lake that widened in the middle.

"You don't sound particularly impressed with your employers' efforts."

"Their efforts? No, I'd have to say I was very impressed by their efforts. No one ever questions their efforts. It was their decision to get involved in the first place."

"You wanted the dam to be built?"

"Everyone wanted the dam to be built, are you kidding? My job is important to me and to my family. Lumber company jobs, those are important to everyone. When the pulp mills are expanding, every business is growing, everyone's working. And the Burkes, well, they'd only been around for a couple of years and had already fought against the building of a mill and then right away they go after this dam. That's them standing in the way of lots of jobs, so that's lots of anger."

"Weren't they acting for good reason, their care for the Ojibway?"

The dam was in clear site, the concrete wall, the buildings on either side, bright white slabs and surfaces in the green wilderness.

"The beaver didn't die. They didn't drown in the flood. Habitat changes all they time. They just moved."

"I understand there was an Ojibway burial ground flooded as well?"

"They blew that way out of proportion. Four graves, from who knows when. I been told they were all grown over. That no one ever visited them."

The pilot flew over the dam compound, then corrected his course to head to Kenora.

"Look, don't get me wrong. I admire Brian and Maureen, and what they're building up here is amazing. Folks flying home after just a couple of days at Innish Cove claim they've been changed, like they've seen what Heaven might be. I see that. But I don't think they understand how many people around here, folks who don't know them as well as I do, well, their first impression of Brian is that he is a self-serving bully and, well, to be honest with you, around here it doesn't help that they're both so...so Irish."

"And I'll toast you the next chance I get when you assure me that you are quick to show your loyalty and set the locals straight."

The two Jameses stood on the porch just outside the front doors of the Great Lodge. They set their tackle boxes on a bench and leaned their rods against the wall. The lawyer removed the envelope from his pocket and turned to the homebuilder.

"You want to give it to her?"

"You want me to give it to her?"

"No, I'm asking if you want to give it to her. Why don't you just go in there and give it to her."

The homebuilder took the envelope just as the door opened and Maureen stepped out, Grace O'Malley holding her right hand, Little Stevie her left.

"Oh, hey, we're on our way to check on you. You need somethin'?"

"Hello, yes, well, we needed to do something. We need to see you… It's our mission."

Maureen stepped up and collected the children in behind her.

"Your mission? Sounds like you're at work in the fields of the Lord."

"I've heard some speak of it that way, yes."

She turned to the children.

"Stevie, take Gracie back to your mother, in the kitchen… Mary… Mary, I'm sendin' the children in to you so keep an eye on them 'til I fetch them," and she nudged the children on their way to Mary who was coming for them, then stepped outside and closed the door behind her.

"It's Kevin who sent us on our mission."

"Kevin?"

"Yes, Kevin."

"You must mean St. Kevin."

"Who?"

"St. Kevin. After St. Patrick, none's more revered."

"Kevin Coogan asked us, as his friends, as your friend, to give this to you."

He held out the envelope for her to take; Maureen didn't reach for it but instead extended both her arms slowly, out to her sides.

"It is said St. Kevin's prayer was so intense, that his prayer was so rich…" With her arms straight out to at her sides now she dropped to her knees in front of the two men. The homebuilder held the envelope out in front of him as he took a step back; the lawyer was frozen in his tracks. "…that one day St. Kevin got down on his knees to pray his love for the Great Creator God an' he became so consumed by his prayer and so transfixed by the power of holy love, he was captured by the fullness of his communion…" She closed her eyes. "Kneeling there, St. Kevin became one with the whole of Creation. He could feel the earth breathing beneath him an' the River was flowing through him, an' the trees were rooted in him, an' he was rooted like a tree in God's love; he could feel it, all of it, pulsin' with the life an' the power of the Great an' Most Holy Spirit as he knelt there, his arms out, lost in prayer, trapped in prayer, as the hours passed, as night came an' then day, an' still he prayed, day after day St. Kevin prayed, out in his hermitage, in his little stone hut he built for prayer, a shelter so small his arms extended out the windows on either side, an' as time passed birds came to perch on his arms an' sang their songs of Creation an' still St. Kevin stayed there, in a deeply blessed communion of the most sacred." Maureen turned her palms up and cupped her fingers. "One day a bird began to build her nest in his hand. Over the days she completed it an' still St. Kevin didn't move, so this mother bird laid her eggs in the nest an' still St. Kevin stayed locked in his inspiration an' his ecstasy an' his deep connection to all that is, an' all that will be 'til finally the baby birds fledged an' flew away an' that's when St. Kevin was released from his holy state to return to his human life a changed man, changed deep, changed forever."

The two Jameses stood quietly as Maureen slowly got to her feet. The homebuilder tried to hand the envelope to her again, and when she wouldn't take it, he tossed it at her feet. She didn't look at it but at them when she spoke again.

"Your Kevin claims he's my friend? You'd think friends was friends because they kept their part of a bargain with their friends. Especially this bargain with this friend."

"Kevin said you'd bring up the bargain and told us to tell you this isn't what you think."

She looked down at the envelope for the first time.

"He says to tell you last year's package was for you but this may be his final plea and our last chance."

With the toe of her boot she flipped the envelope back towards them.

"You can return it to Kevin, the seal intact. Tell him I burned the first, unread, an' sent the ashes to the wind."

The lawyer turned to leave and touched the homebuilder by the arm for him to come too, leaving the envelope on the ground at her feet.

"I'm sorry but our loyalties are with Kevin. So there it is. We've delivered it to you. We're here for three days if you have any questions about what's in there, or if you have any messages you want us to send to Kevin for you."

"I'd have you on a plane in two hours if I wanted you out of camp, an' you'd best be clear about that. An' if I ever have anythin' to say to Kevin, I'll be deliverin' it meself."

Maureen followed the path towards her house but kept going, climbing the narrow path behind the house up a short, steep slope to a rocky lip of a ledge that looked over the whole scene; over their home and the Great Lodge, and the cabins and office, and storehouses and sheds, and ice house and bunkhouse, and beach and dock, and Innish Cove and the narrow finger of land that protected the cove and separated it from Rainbow Lake and the River.

At the small cleared ledge Brian had shaped a bench from a fallen log and it sat just back from the edge of rock. Maureen passed the bench and kept climbing, forging her own path another ten yards up the slope, where she stopped to kneel at a gnarled pine whose twisted roots created a hollow hidden from the bench. She pulled from inside her shirt the large manila envelope the two Jameses left with her, then reached into the hollow to remove a similar envelope. She returned to the bench with both of them and broke the seal on the first, one she had hidden unread when it was delivered late last season by a guest from Boston, who also claimed to be Kevin's friend and hers. She hadn't been ready for that one.

She spread the contents of this first envelope over the bench. An extract of a University study, comparing the increase of Protestant economic success with the continued Catholic poverty in the Northern Counties, proved to be the thickest portion. "Last 30 years the Gap's widen" was written on the cover of the study in the thick pencil strokes Maureen thought she recognized as Kevin's hand.

There was a newspaper article from *The United Irishman*, reporting on Operation Harvest and quoting IRA leaders' call for support for this campaign, at home and abroad. One bit of the article had been circled in that same thick pencil and Maureen felt the cool dark lead with her fingers. She read some of it, and her lips moved, and soon she was reading softly aloud.

"....so what gave rise to feelin's of hope about the Ebrington Barracks raid was not the capture of some guns, though that was important, it was not to make the British Army look foolish, though that was most grand, it was not merely a spectacular operation, though it was certainly that. It was the illumination of the indisputable fact that the British Army of Occupation is still in Ireland, that it still holds Irish territory by force of arms long after the case has been made that armed occupation is an act of war, an' every international authority agrees with the citizens' right to defend his country against acts of war."

Stuck inside the envelope she found a personal letter from Kevin; the pencil strokes confirmed the others had been his. He was hoping to find her well and asked about Brian and Grace O'Malley. He told her that the leadership she could provide was badly needed, and asked her to consider joining Operation Harvest. At the end of the letter he wrote:

"I've long warned you against seeking revenge. We should pursue a measured justice, that's been my view, though I find it harder and harder to rally others to it. My dear Maureen, I mention this last for I feel I must tell you we have an informant who promises he can find us the name of the Black and Tan who pulled the trigger on the pistol that killed the Irish hero and true Fenian Donovan O'Toole, may he rest in Peace. Please get word to me soon, as the lead is most fresh, for if you wish us to pursue with diligence, discovering the identity and location of the man who killed your father, we shall."

Maureen's hands began to shake as she read this last paragraph again, and again, then one more time. Her eyes watered while she looked out to the East, this time past the far ridges; she looked all the way East to Ireland as she said a prayer for her father.

"In the name of St. Patrick, an' of St. Kevin, an' of St. Brendan, I pray for the Lord's sword of justice for me da, Donovan O'Toole. In the Lord's right hand may it be swift an' true." She paused a long moment, then continued in prayer. "An' if it must be that I am that sword, well, that seems a true sort of justice to me, in accordance with Your will, Amen."

She returned the contents to the envelope, then picked up the second, folded both envelopes together, and with them tucked in the top of her pants at the small of her back she climbed back down the slope to her home.

After riding most of the morning, Joe Loon turned the boat to the shore where his trap line led along the ridge to the dam. Simon carried the knapsack, hung over one shoulder, and followed Brian, who followed Joe Loon, through the trees on a diagonal climb up the low ridge. They hiked for most of an hour, stopping when Joe Loon examined a fresh wind fall or hollow tree as a marten trap site, and they spoke very little as they walked on until they crested a second taller ridge and looked down on the new dam and the powerhouse, and the flooded forest valley behind it.

At the top of the ridge, at the best viewpoint, This Man stood watching and waiting. He was dressed and painted as Raven Master, the top half of his face black, the bottom half yellow with white stripes, black feathers fanned flat on the top of his head; he wore a beaded buckskin shirt and black and white leggings.

Joe Loon stood next to This Man and Brian and Simon joined him. The lake that formed behind the dam changed the valley so completely that Simon did not recognize it; he knew the abandoned burial site was flooded somewhere on the far side of the lake but didn't know where. Brian had little familiarity with this River valley; it was far enough from Innish Cove that he had only visited it once, with Maureen and Simon, and Albert Loon, as they mounted their last ditch effort to slow down the construction; Albert wanted them to see the old burial site with its four graves.

When Brian compared the half completed dam with the broken down grave markers, he knew their efforts were futile.

After a few moments, and in the same instant, Joe Loon and This Man began soft low chants, but to very different purposes. Joe Loon's was a farewell song and when Simon heard this he joined his Grandfather. But This Man sang a song that beckoned. His was a song of greeting; he was waiting for visitors still to come.

After Joe Loon said farewell to the world that was gone, he listened for any word of where the big beaver were, now that the River shore and feeder creeks and forest shelf where they had lived was flooded by the newly formed lake. He stood there a long time, silently. They were all quiet, but Joe Loon did not hear any whispers from the spirits or from his ancestors about what was happening here now.

They were hungry. Simon removed sandwiches and apples and cookies and cold broiled chicken breasts and two bottles of beer and a bottle of Coke from the knapsack. They ate, sitting together, This Man sitting off a bit, chanting his welcoming prayer, holding a large eagle feather in his red-painted hands and pointing it to the East, then the South, then the West, then to the North, presenting his bag of magic to the Four Directions when the prayers called for it.

After his meal Joe Loon stood at the edge of the ridge top, his back to the others, facing the dam. Simon told Brian what Joe Loon said.

"I understand this now. The white man is also a trapper. He traps the fire power from the River…"

He looked at the power lines that cut through the forest, snaking their way south.

"…The fire power of this River is mighty. The white man is smart. He has learned how to trap this fire to shoot its power through these lines to their villages and to their homes."

He turned to the north, to watch the River's course below the dam.

"The power of Gitche Manitou is great. When the River rounds the first bend below the dam the water power of the River has returned."

He turned to study the lake again but a sudden horn blast, a loud round sound coming from the dam, interrupted him, and then it blasted again, then again. Simon and Brian stood at the horn blasts, and as the last one faded they watched the dam's spill gates open and a massive surge of four waterfalls poured out into the River below the dam.

Simon turned to his grandfather to gauge his reaction. Joe Loon was concerned.

"Grandfather. The shore line behind the dam will move now."

"If some of the time the water is high, and some of the time the water is low, that will make it much harder for the big beaver to learn how to make their home here. It will make it much harder for me to learn what is happening here now."

The sun set and rose again, and it was near dusk in the world of dams and fishing camps when This Man greeted the visitors he had been waiting for from the next world.

Hunter came first, from out of the West. He carried the bow and arrow he used to shoot three arrows into the side of the big bull moose that kept his village alive one terribly cold winter.

Young Sister came from the South. In one hand she held a doll of woven willow, and clutched in her other hand were the child-sized eating utensils she was learning to make.

Grandmother came from the North. She carried her weaving frame strapped to her back and her best birch basket under her arm.

Trapper came from the East. Slung over his shoulder was his first Hudson Bay trap, and a killing club hung from his waist.

The items each of the travelers carried were laid upon their graves by their families for use in the next world.

As the travelers gathered around This Man, they sang the same farewell that Joe Loon had sung the day before in his world.

Maureen avoided the two Jameses when they were in camp; the night before they were to fly home, at two in the morning when the camp was sleeping, she made her way in the dark forest to the Chapel to recover the bundle she had hidden there earlier in the evening. With the bundle tucked inside her jacket she followed the path that led through the forest, past the quiet cabins, to the beach, to the office and storage sheds at the foot of the dock. She walked past the dock to the icehouse sitting on a short rocky ledge. She opened the big walk-in icebox and found two cardboard boxes of fish fillets marked Conaty and two marked Brislanne; she removed one of each. She cut open the tape, removed half the wrapped fillets, and slipped something from the bundle into one box and then the other. She repacked the boxes, taped them up again, and returned them to the freezer.

❆ ❆ ❆

The next afternoon at the Minneapolis airport the two Jameses claimed their luggage and boxes of fish and lined up to clear customs.

"She's something else."

"Best I could tell we got no less service than any other guest."

"But nothing for Kevin except she claims to have burned his first package and we saw her in the vicinity of his second package, and when we went to the same spot later that day it was gone. She had to pick it up. She couldn't let anyone else find it."

"But she probably burned it, too."

The two Jameses were next in line. Operating on a tip phoned in that morning, the U.S. Customs officers asked if they could inspect their luggage and boxes of fish.

"Its limits of walleye and northern pike and a couple of smallmouth bass, all packed in camp."

"And we got dry ice in Kenora."

"Yes, sir. What I am saying is I would like to open these boxes and determine the contents for myself and so I am asking if I can report that you cooperated and gave me your permission."

"Sure, go ahead."

The Jameses hadn't noticed the presence of other men in uniforms close by, two with pistols holstered at their sides, but now the lawyer did.

"I should say, we did not pack these boxes in camp, but rather our guides did, I guess it's them, unless she…"

Two customs officials opened the boxes and removed the shiny brown butcher paper packages of frozen fillets, stacking them. One stopped and called the other over. A uniformed man with a side arm joined them. When he saw what was inside the box his nod called the other armed man to attention behind the two Jameses who could see it coming.

"…unless she… that goddamn bitch."

The officials picked up the boxes, the senior official led the way, and they all followed, the homebuilder shaking his head, a wry smile barely there, the attorney explaining that he was a lawyer, so they were advised to do whatever was about to happen with full respect for their legal rights.

They were led to a room with a table and some chairs, then left alone. After a few minutes the area supervisor and the shift leader entered; two men with side arms stood by the door. The shift leader placed two boxes on the table, and they sat down across from the two Jameses.

"What do you think we found in two of your boxes?"

"Fish."

"What else?"

"I'm sure if you contacted Brian Burke at The Great Lodge at Innish Cove he would tell you they don't allow their guests to clean their own fish or pack them. They insisted on doing that for us."

"And then the boxes are in your possession for, what, hours certainly, before you arrive here. They had clearly been opened and then taped closed a second time."

"What did that bitch put in there?"

"And who is this person you refer to so unpleasantly?"

The homebuilder was sure the lawyer had made a mistake, so he took over.

"The Indian girl who actually boxes the fish up, after the guides fillet the fish she wraps 'em up and boxes 'em. Well, she wasn't bad looking for an Indian fish girl and my friend here had too much to drink one night and I guess you could say he kind of insulted her honor, said something stupid to her, but he'd been drinking all day and when he drinks, he acts like an asshole."

The supervisor reached into the boxes and pulled out two pistols, Colt .45s.

"You must have been quite an asshole. This morning we get a tip. About guns. And we find you with these, which leads to some very interesting questions."

The attorney was grateful his partner had saved him and was back on his game.

"Like, why does anyone need to smuggle guns into the United States?"

"Okay, we can start there. Why would you smuggle guns into the United States?"

"My point is we don't need to. We can buy them. So we'll answer each and every one of your questions to the best of our ability and with complete transparency, which is just going to frustrate you, because how they got there is just as big a mystery to us as it is to you. And if there's a fine, we'll pay it, or you just confiscate the guns…"

"I assure you, the guns are confiscated."

"Please, ask your questions so you can assure yourselves there's nothing to learn from us, but keep in mind that so many folks have access to these boxes there is no way you can accuse us of anything other than being in the wrong place at the wrong time."

"Sure. You know your rights and we've no case and the fucking bitch is really an Indian girl who won't fuck." He pushed his chair back and stood. "Just let me consult with Officer Brown and we'll be right back to talk about how we need to proceed here."

They left the room and closed the door behind them. Officer Brown said, "He's right you know. We can fine them for carrying a concealed weapon but there's nothing else to make of this."

"I know. But he's being such a mick asshole, let's just let 'em sit in there for a while. I'm behind on some paper work."

Chapter 3
THIS MAN BRINGS FIRE TO THE PEOPLE

JOE LOON'S CLAN camped at Innish Cove the first three years of the fishing camps operation. By then the fishing camp had grown so large, that each season thereafter the clan returned to the place on the bank of the River where their village was the day Brian and Maureen first arrived to scout the area, on the shores of a shallow cove just a couple of miles north of Innish Cove. The village was also growing, as steady employment at Big Brian's camp attracted other families. Many were Loon clan members, many were Sturgeon clan members, and all were welcome. They came and they went, some families staying for a few weeks, others for the full season.

On this evening everyone living in the village followed the path that led through the grove of trees behind the cluster of tents and wigwams to the fire circle at the base of a granite ridge, at the foot of a wide flat rock wall.

The men sat close to Joe Loon, the women gathered together across the way, the youngest with their mothers, the oldest sons with their fathers and uncles, the rest of the children in their own groups, all around the blazing fire.

Joe Loon told a story to everyone gathered that night while the fire threw dancing shadows on the rock wall. Those shadows soon became the images of the story Joe Loon told for Little Stevie and then for Old George.

"The story of how This Man brought Fire to his people. One day before our ancestors' time, This Man asked Nokomis why the people must suffer from the terrible cold all winter. He wanted to find some way for his people to stay warm through the long dark winters.

"Nokomis told This Man the stories she knew of a place far away where an old man had the gift of warmth. He called this gift Fire. But he was a selfish old man. That is why he lived in a land far away from the Original people. He refused to share Fire with anyone else. He wanted to keep it for himself and his daughters.

"This Man told Nokomis he would journey to this land to get Fire from the old man to bring back to his people. Nokomis was afraid when she heard this. She did not want This Man to travel alone so far from his village. She told him to stay with her. But he was determined to go. She wished him well as he set off. As This Man left their village, he told Nokomis to be ready with the kindling when he returned.

"This Man walked for many days. He walked for many moons. He traveled through the forests and across the great plains. He climbed many mountains and swam across many great lakes. When he came close to the lodge of the old man, he hid behind a bush to think of a plan to get inside the old man's lodge. He saw a rabbit running by and he decided to change himself into a rabbit, so when the old man's daughters saw him they would feel sorry for him and they would carry him inside to protect him from the cold.

"This Man's plan worked, for the youngest daughter saw the rabbit shivering in the snow and she ran out and tucked him under her robe to carry him inside. The old man was very angry when he saw what his daughter had done. He did not allow any strange creatures in his lodge house, not even a tired rabbit. But the old man was weary in the warmth of his Fire and soon he fell asleep. The daughters put the rabbit near Fire to warm himself and left him there as they set out to prepare their father's meal. As soon as the daughters turned away Fire cracked and popped and the rabbit dashed forward to catch a Fire spark on his back. When the daughters saw this they knew they had been tricked. They called for their father, but by then the rabbit had run out the door and over the snowy meadow into the woods and was gone.

"As rabbit, This Man ran for many days, the spark of Fire on his back. When he neared his village he called to Nokomis to have the kindling ready. She did. She took the spark of Fire from the rabbit's back and soon had Fire burning, warming their lodge.

"Now the rabbit changed back to This Man. He went outside to call all the people to come and take a spark from his Fire. The people were glad to learn they would be able to keep their children and themselves warm through the long cold winters."

❋ ❋ ❋

Joe Loon's wife, Naomi, stood over the fire. They had allowed it to burn down as the night went on, but now she was shaping it for one last good burn, feeding it sticks and two small logs, enjoying the heat on her skin and the rise of her blood. As she tended the fire, the last of the old men and old women stood and headed down the path through the forest, two lanterns marking their progress through the trees to the village.

When she turned from her labor she was alone with her husband.

Until then Joe Loon had been sitting with the elders, discussing village matters, listening to news about the new dam changing life on the River for an upstream clan, and sharing stories about recent guests at Innish Cove. Naomi sat next to her husband now as he relaxed from the strong posture a chief elder assumed when others were with him at the fire; he met his wife's body with his as they settled in next to each other.

As the new logs began to blaze Joe Loon and Naomi scooted forward, closer to the fire. The fire warmed both their faces now and tightened the skin. They edged closer still, each smiling at what was to come. Joe Loon put his arm behind his wife, and she leaned into his chest. He pulled the blanket they were sitting on up over their shoulders while slowly but deliberately her free hand worked through layers of his clothes to find his offering, and his free hand unfolded hers, and the heat of the fire stoked their passions.

Chapter 4
PLANS MADE

BRIAN AND MAUREEN WERE IN BED, in the middle of the night. He breathed steadily, making the sounds Maureen knew came from his deepest sleep. She listened, waited longer still, then slipped from between the sheets and pushed her pillows up against Brian as she left him. She pulled on her robe and stepped softly into the hall.

She stopped at the door of her daughter's bedroom.

She was sleeping peacefully. The rocking chair next to her bed was caught in the full moon's glow through the window. Maureen settled into the chair, watching her daughter sleep, and she slowly rocked in the moonlight, humming an Irish lullaby.

After a few moments Maureen leaned forward, her face was so near her daughter's she could smell her breath. She poked her hand between the mattresses, burying her arm to her shoulder before she pulled it back, holding the two envelopes that she taped together before she hid them there. She leaned back in the chair and opened the second package, looking straightaway for another letter from Kevin, and finding it tucked in another edition of *The United Irishman*.

In the moonlight she quickly scanned Kevin's letter for mention of her father's name, found none, then read it carefully. Kevin skipped any personal message this time and was insistent that right now was the last chance to drive the British out of the North. He was asking her to come lead a flying column, or assist in training, but in any case they needed the support of all their best right now, or the cause was lost; the Six Counties would be part of Great Britain, forever.

A section of an article was circled on the front page of the newspaper. It wasn't in Kevin's familiar heavy pencil, but rather in black ink, and Maureen wasn't sure if it was Kevin's hand or not.

The circled lines read, "This is the age old struggle of the Irish people versus British occupation. This is the cause for which generations of our people have sacrificed their lives, have suffered and died…" Someone had written "D O'Toole's murderer located" in very small letters in the margin next to that line; instantly the tears began to form, and again she said a quick prayer for a peaceful rest and final justice for her da, then she continued reading. "… In this grave hour, all Irish men and women, at home and abroad, must set aside all differences, political or religious, and rally behind the banner of national liberation…"

But she found they were just words, empty words that meant nothing to her, for she couldn't stop thinking about what she would do if she had a gun in her hand with the Black and Tan who shot her da standing in front of her. She turned her back on her daughter and held an imaginary pistol in her hands, aimed at the murderer's forehead, and without hesitation she fired, miming with satisfaction the recoil of the shot. She turned back in her chair, and rocked and rocked.

After a few minutes she picked up the paper from her lap and skimmed it, looking for names she knew and finding but a few. She reread Kevin's letter, then returned the contents to the envelope, the envelopes to the hiding place. She kissed her daughter's forehead before she backed out of the room, watching Grace sleep as she went. She climbed back in bed with Brian.

"Everythin' okay?"

"I was just checkin' on Gracie."

❋ ❋ ❋

There was but a week left in the fishing season. Albert had said something to Maureen during the previous hunting season that she and Brian interpreted as Joe Loon growing tired of the trophy killing of black bear and moose by the white man, so they decided to take a year off from booking any hunting parties. While they served their guests they were also preparing the camp for the winter. Half the cabins were empty and being cleaned and closed by Mary and her crew. Not an hour earlier Dutch had flown in with the last party of the season, four manufacturer reps from Chicago.

The guests had just left to fish the River's lakes with their guides.

Brian and Maureen were returning with Dutch to Kenora for the day to tend to various business matters. Simon continued the practice of traveling with them regularly, when it seemed it might be a trip that could teach him about the white man and how he thinks. They boarded the Norseman as Dutch started the engine. To say goodbye to her parents Grace was allowed on the dock, and she stood there with Mary and Little Stevie and waved goodbye to her ma and da as the plane taxied out of the cove. Grace waited for the plane to soar over the lake and disappear behind the far ridge before they turned to walk back down the dock to shore. Half way down the dock, Grace O'Malley began to run, and Little Stevie ran after her.

When they passed the ridge Dutch told Brian to remove the papers from the satchel behind his chair, and after Brian examined them and asked Dutch a couple of clarifying questions, he joined Maureen and Simon on the bench seats along the cargo hold.

"The Dutchman put this together for us. Looks very interesting."

He handed the papers to his wife.

"If we buy that Otter the boys at de Havilland are not only droppin' the price another ten percent, but if we sign before our trip to Chicago they'll rent us a plane for the trip at their basic operating costs. Dutch says he'll fly us, which means he comes too, all for almost half of what our commercial flights cost just you and me last year. Plus the Dutchman is there so we can take some breaks."

Maureen had seen the numbers. Dutch asked her advice as he was building them. She didn't indicate her familiarity as she studied them now.

"An' you're urgin' a go ahead?"

"Me an' you flyin' into Chicago with our own pilot? Sounds grand. We've been talkin' about gettin' an Otter for a couple of years now an' this is very competitive pricin'." Maureen was quiet. "An' imagine introducin' our blues club to Dutch."

"I thought when we bought the Goose you said it was instead of an Otter."

"Ahhh, you must admit our guests love that extra comfort the Goose offers."

"But they won't pay extra for it, an' it costs more to operate."

"We're quite profitable when we carry four or more passengers."

"Which happens how often? Hey Dutch, how often would you say Tony flies the Goose in with four or more passengers?"

"Close to half the time, eh?"

"I've checked. It's barely a third of the time. The rest of the time, the Goose flies at our cost, at our loss."

Brian had expected her enthusiasm and was confused with her steadily growing dismissal.

"What's wrong here? From the beginnin' you've been pushin' for more growth. An' we grow every year, some years faster than others, but it's the safest bet I know that we'll grow again next year an' the one after, amen."

"Lately I find I've been tryin' on a new business perspective, seein' the world through a different set of priorities, yeah. Maybe instead a investin' all our profits back into expandin' the businesses, maybe it's time we start runnin' them for maximum profits and start savin' some, start puttin' somethin' aside, for tomorrow, for contingencies."

"For Gracie girl."

"That's right, an' for you an' for me."

"We'll start at savin' soon enough. We need two more cabins for a neat dozen, an' if one of them is that big cabin you designed last winter that'll give us a capacity of 60 guests an' if I say there's been plenty of times we could have been filled at that level if we had the space you'll say..."

"Plenty of times? For a few days is more like it."

Brian shook his head. "Well, I've been promisin' the Bachelor boys from Grassy Narrows we'd build another guide bunkhouse so we gotta do that. An' we need a larger electric generator. An' this Otter...Come on, the fun is in the growin' of it; you've said so time an' again."

"The profit is in gettin' the most from what we've built." Brian didn't like to show his disappointment in her in front of Simon, but Maureen could see it and decided it was time.

"What if I didn't go on your trip to Chicago?"

"*My* trip?"

"Then there is just your plane ticket to pay for, so. Then we can take our time considerin' the purchase of another plane, yeah, an' wait an' see what next year looks like."

"An' why wouldn't you come? These shows, we've always done 'em together."

"Always? This will be our third year."

"But why would you miss a return to our blues club?"

"Because the same time the shows are takin' place, well, it happens to be the best time for me to visit Mum."

"She's fine?"

"Besides her cottage is just outside Derry an' so she lives with British oppression every day? Sorry, yes, she's all right."

"Yes, sure, you need to go an' check on her, an' then finally convince her to come live with us."

"She's a stubborn woman who believes hell ain't fire but two feet of snow."

"Go over an' try, but come with me, too. You can do both. We can do both."

"The show in Chicago is Mum's birthday, an' the next day is my niece's first Holy Communion. It's been seven years since I've seen Mum on her birthday an' the Lord knows how many family communions I've missed."

Brian was quiet, thinking, no longer trying to hide his disappointment.

"What would we do with Gracie?"

"I've thought about that. She'd come with me and I would leave her with her Uncle Eamon when I visit Mum."

"Sure they'd love to see her. This feels like one of those times you've decided already?"

"I'm not ignorin' your concerns, but yes, I've decided already."

❋ ❋ ❋

Mary was in the kitchen, peeling potatoes. Grace O'Malley and

Little Stevie were under the table, playing with their bits and pieces. Grace picked up a piece of driftwood and lay back on the pillow that sat on a small blanket. She held the piece of wood in front of her eyes, and turned it, watching one surface flow into another. Little Stevie climbed the carved lynx he was playing with over stones and pine cones, and it leapt over Grace's shoe, then he brought the lynx with him as he laid his head on the pillow next to hers, shoulder to shoulder. He reached over to kiss Grace's driftwood with his lynx and she kissed the lynx with her driftwood.

After a couple of minutes passed Mary checked to see why the children were so quiet. She found them both asleep, each curled in a ball, facing one another, the driftwood in Little Stevie's hand, the lynx hiding in a tangle of Grace's hair.

Simon's new practice was to separate himself from Brian and Maureen when they walked the streets of Kenora on business, usually five yards ahead. When he told his reasons to Maureen she was proud of him. "I want to see if I can stand alone in the white man's world."

He led them up the slope of land above the NOA office at the float plane docks on Lake of the Woods onto the sidewalk leading to downtown. They approached a corner where a drunken Ojibway sat alone. Simon walked past whispering a prayer that the spirits that haunted the man would allow him some rest.

Brian slowed a step and asked his wife, "Do we know this fella?"

"When they are so into the drink, nothin' about them is recognizable. They're very much like the Celts that way, yeah."

Brian took out his wallet for the dollar he would hand in response to the drunken appeal. He handed it to the man as they continued on their way.

But Brian was recognized.

"Big Brian g'me a dolla."

Brian stopped to look again at who this was but couldn't identify him. Many Grassy Narrows and White Dog Reserve Ojibway tried guiding and didn't like it and didn't stay long enough for Brian to learn who they were.

"Big Bri' a great friend of Ojibway. Everyone knows this is

so. That is why Big Bri' give me a dollar. But what can I do wit'a a fuckin' dolla, eh?"

Maureen took Brian's arm when she saw he bristled at the disregard.

"The situation has one successful resolution. You keep walkin'."

"Why did he say that?"

"Don't judge or you'll be judged."

With the next corner turned, they were downtown, headed to their attorney's office. Off the lobby of the office building there was a travel agent, and Maureen stopped at the door that Simon had just entered.

"You two go on up. I'm going to see about flights, then I'll join you."

❇ ❇ ❇

The Great Lodge at Innish Cove had just closed for the winter; it was boarded up and put away. Joe Loon's clan would stay in their village for a few more weeks and Albert would check on Innish Cove one more time before the clan packed up to travel to Grassy Narrows as their winter camp. Brian had a practice of flying in with Dutch for one last check in the final days the River was ice free; Maureen teased him that he needed to give Innish Cove one last goodnight kiss for the long winter nap.

Brian was at the dock with the stack of family luggage, waiting for Dutch to fly in to take them to town. Maureen and Grace O'Malley were in the Chapel, sitting side by side in front of the statue.

"He's my age."

Maureen was lost in a searching prayer; Grace touched her arm.

"Is he my age?"

She heard her daughter this time.

"Who?"

Grace pointed to the boy climbing his father's shoulder. "Jesus."

Maureen looked up. The boy could be five, but Maureen had imagined him younger. Since Grace was small for her age they looked the same age.

"I guess so."

"I don't like our house in Kenora, Mum."

"What?"

"I don't want to live in Kenora."

"I've never heard you say that before. Why don't you want to live there?"

"Because Little Stevie and all my friends are here."

"We wouldn't see them durin' the winter if we stayed. They go live at Grassy Narrows now."

"Then I want to go live there, too."

Maureen smiled and wished Brian was there to hear this for himself.

"We can't do that sweetheart. Only Ojibway live at Grassy Narrows."

"We should ask them. I think they want us to live there with them."

"We need to live in town, Gracie. But I tell you what. Maybe it's time for you to go to school. You'd make lots of friends in school."

The suggestion brought fear to her daughter's eyes.

"Little Stevie says the schools are *scary*. They hit the children at school, with sticks and with belts and they make them bleed."

"Oh no, Gracie girl, he's talkin' about a very different sort of school that they only send the Indian children to. At *your* school the teachers would be very nice. I promise you. They would never hurt any of their students."

"Little Stevie is afraid someday he will get caught by the bad men who want to send him to school."

"I will go with you an' show you the school I am talkin' about, yeah, an' if you don't want to go I won't make you."

"Okay."

Grace sat quietly, but she was determined to convince her mother to let her live with her Ojibway friends.

"Are you sure only Ojibway live at Grassy Narrows?"

"Yes, I am. But maybe this winter your father an' I can take you to visit Little Stevie there."

"Yes, please."

"I'll work on it."

Maureen thought for a moment about how this place, here in front of the statute, had become her home, the place she felt most at rest. Then she returned to her prayer, searching for guidance in her response to Kevin's call, for forgiveness for deceiving her husband about the nature of her trip, and asking the Lord God Almighty what her role must be to get justice for her father.

"An' may God bless the Innocents."

Chapter 5
WINTER WONDER

IT WAS CHRISTMAS EVE in the early dawn and the world was covered in snow, blanketed with snow, shrouded and capped by snow. Brian, Maureen, and Grace O'Malley drove their '55 Ford Country Squire station wagon through the deserted streets of Kenora; the streetlights were still on. Brian was at the wheel, controlling the car's slide as he turned a corner to head north on Highway 678, a two lane highway, plowed and cleared. So much snow had already fallen that winter that in many places the plows created snow walls on both sides of the highway nearly twice as high as the roof of the car.

Maureen sat next to Brian, and Grace O'Malley stood on the back seat, leaning forward to rest her elbows on the back of the front seat between her parents; she was dressed for an adventure in the snow and calling out with laughter whenever the car slid on a slippery bit of pavement. She sang absent-mindedly. Often the lyrics were nothing more than "Little Stevie, Little Stevie" sung to her own tune.

"Little Stevie sure will be happy to see me."

"He will indeed."

Dutch was waiting for Brian and his family further north on the highway where a logging road provided access to the River. Dutch had been working for days to arrange the transportation for an adventurous trip over the River and through the woods and the deep snow to Grassy Narrows Reserve.

The tailgate of the station wagon was filled with Christmas presents the Burkes were bringing to their friends on the Reserve. Many of the gifts were for Joe Loon's clan. As the fishing camp grew Brian hired more and more guides from the men whose families had years before moved fulltime to the Reserve—when they guided the men lived in the Bachelor's Bunkhouse Brian built for them at Innish Cove—and he had presents for the regular Bachelor's as well.

They drove north for most of an hour, rounded a turn, and up ahead they saw the curved lines of the dark blue Bombardier half-track against the snow and pines. The enclosed twelve-passenger snow machine—skis in the front, Caterpillar tracks wrapped around a series of five wheels—was heated and stocked with food and warm drinks, blankets, and plenty of extra fuel stored safely. They exchanged Christmas greetings, caught up with news as they loaded the gifts from the station wagon, and then Dutch showed Brian and Maureen how to operate the snow machine's controls in its solo cockpit.

They said thanks and goodbye and Merry Christmas to Dutch, agreed to meet there at noon the day after Christmas, and Dutch left in the station wagon as Brian took off through the forest down the logging road that led to a feeder branch of the River. He traveled an easy pace at first, slowly increasing his speed as Maureen's teasing urged and as he grew more confident steering the skis in the deep snow.

Grace O'Malley stood on the seat next to her mother and looked out the round window as the Bombardier knocked the snow-covered fir branches that tossed their snow into the sunlight and then danced for her in their brilliant silver shower. Her sing-song tune changed and she began to sing, in Irish Gaelic, *Silent Night*. After the third line she faltered, so Maureen, and then Brian joined her, and their voices carried her along.

"*Oíche Chiúin, oíche Mhic Dé, Cách 'na suan, dís araon, Dís is dílse 'faire le spéire,*

Naíon beag gnaoigheal ceannanntais caomh..."

They sang as they sped through the forest but stopped when Brian slowed down as he approached the River. He looked out over the snow-covered, ice-covered River.

"It's frozen a month?"

Maureen leaned forward to look out over Brian's shoulder.

"It's thick enough. Let's go."

"Shouldn't I check it?"

"The Mounties been takin' their Bombardiers on the River for over two weeks, yeah."

"How do you know that?"

"Dutch called them for me an' asked."

Brian opened his door as he eased the Bombardier down the bank onto the frozen River. He turned off the engine and listened. He got out and brushed back the snow to see the ice, to judge its thickness, and it was solid, neither sign nor sound of cracking. Except the wind and his own sounds all was quiet, until Grace O'Malley said, "Da, Little Stevie is wondering where I am," and Maureen laughed. Brian got back in, started the engine, engaged the track, and headed off down the River.

This branch of the River wound its way through the vast spruce forests before it joined up with other branches to form a main channel that would lead through ridges before it opened into a wide lake. On the far side of that lake sat Grassy Narrows Reserve, where a full River channel formed again. The directions were clear and the distances were great, so Brian sped down the River at full throttle.

At first they found places where sections of the forest had been logged recently by pulp companies and others where the logging was years before and the forest was restoring itself.

When they arrived at the main River channel, much of the ice was wind swept of snow. When they left the main channel they plowed back into the deeper snow caught between the ridges, and once they faltered in a deep drift but Brian found the best-geared power to plow through.

The ridges gave way, the channel got broader, and they came out upon the lake. Here, too, the wind had control, and they saw that most of the lake's blue grey ice ahead of them had been swept clear of snow by the steady wind and strong gusts. Brian was practiced on ice by now, and they flew across the lake on the smooth clean sheet. Grace studied it from the window and then declared, "Da. I want to play on the ice."

"I do, too, Bri. Look at how beautiful it is. We're on an adventure, remember?"

"Let's just get a bit closer to the far shore an' block some of that wind."

They traveled on but soon Maureen told Brian to stop. She made sure her daughter was bundled well, and they stepped out onto the ice. Grace O'Malley ran and slid, and ran and slid, and fell, and when she fell she found she could slide better on her knees than her rubber-soled boots and she did, running and running and then dropping to her knees to slide and make her parents laugh as she did it over and over again.

On her hands and knees she invested a deep attention studying the patterns of bubbles and small cracks captured in the thick sheet of ice. Brian had turned off the Bombardier's engine so they could enjoy the full silence of the deep north wood's winter.

Her parents laughed some more when Grace hopped up again, and ran and slid and fell and slid. While she was on her knees, Maureen bent down to take her shoulders and pushed her along like a sled, and Grace O'Malley called, "Faster Momma, faster." Maureen took two quick steps then let go with a last forceful and measured push so Grace slid and slid and slid, slowly turning as she did, and then she stopped, facing the far shore fifty yards away. Their laughter filled the space around them.

They became suddenly silent.

First the deer, a mature doe, stumbled from the trees, trying to run, but struggling in the deep snow from her obvious exhaustion, trying to leap but never fully clearing the drifts, fighting her way towards the shore and finally busting out of the snow and jumping out onto the ice. Brian started to laugh when the deer hit the ice, for her legs flew out from under her and she fell, her legs splayed. But Maureen and Grace O'Malley sucked their breath, for they had sensed something else was coming. As the deer struggled to get to her feet Brian sensed it, too, just before they saw what had panicked the doe.

Two wolves stepped out together, one grey and white, the other midnight black, and they stood side by side on a small bit of high ground over the shore, their heads held low, tongues hanging, panting, looking down at the struggling deer, seemingly ignoring the family. Maureen took a moment to notice the wolves' patience, as if they knew the mission was now accomplished, before she ran to Grace O'Malley, slipped and fell into her, and scrambled to get up. As she grabbed her daughter two more wolves ran out onto the ice from under the branches of the pines closest to shore, and they attacked the deer together while the doe was still down, one wolf taking a hind leg, the black one biting at the deer's neck until it found a firm grip. Maureen thought Grace must have seen the rush of the initial attack but only heard the snarling and the bleating of the killing as she turned with her, slipping and nearly falling again.

Brian was behind the controls of the Bombardier, the engine on, the side door open for Maureen to jump in. After they settled he headed the snow craft right at the wolves, intending to drive them off. Maureen had been looking down at Grace to make sure she had her view of the scene obscured. When she noted his course she asked "Whatta' ya doin'?"

"I'm gonna chase 'em away."

The wolves looked up when they realized the machine was coming closer.

"They're wolves, Brian. Wolves kill deer."

Three wolves stepped back from the kill but the black one stood his ground, first blood stains on their muzzles, growls curling their lips.

Brian veered off to head towards the shore where he expected to find the River branch that would take them the final distance to the Reserve. Maureen turned to watch the wolves hunker down to their kill, keeping the view blocked for Grace, but studying it herself until it was too far behind them.

After one false start they found the right branch and sped along. Grace sat still in her mother's lap. No one spoke about what they had witnessed. As they followed the winding branch, Maureen felt her daughter relax, and then cuddle, and finally she fell asleep. She created a bed for her daughter on the floor with some blankets as Brian sped down the snow-covered River towards their destination. After tucking a blanket around their daughter, Maureen leaned forward and announced she'd like to drive, so they stopped to change places; it was Maureen's cockpit now, and Brian settled in the back with their daughter.

As she took over the controls Maureen said "I've been thinkin' about my trip to see Mum. What if I asked Mary Fobister to come with me to help me care for Grace?"

"Mary with you an' Gracie in Ireland. That's a picture."

The Bombardier rounded a wide bend and again the snow was deep so they plowed through as they drove over.

"Eamon is the best of the best an' sure Grace loves the idea of Katie an' Tommy—"

"That's the only thing Patrick is doin' that angers me, that he won't meet Gracie. She is his sister."

"Well if you aren't there with her maybe he will."

Maureen was quiet while Brian considered that possibility with a smile.

"So Grace loves them, but they're strangers, yeah, an' she looks to Mary as her second mother. I have no way of knowin' how long I might need to be with Mum; especially if she decides to come live here, I'll be attendin' to arrangements an' that takes time and attention."

They rounded another bend and Brian saw a wisp of smoke drifting above the trees ahead of them.

"See it?"

"Must be Grassy Narrows."

They stopped again so Brian would be driving when they arrived. Maureen attended to their daughter, kneeling down to gently wake her.

"Gracie. Gracie. We're here honey."

Grace O'Malley jumped up and climbed the seat to look out the porthole. She wasn't satisfied with her view—she didn't see anyone—so climbed back down to lean into the cockpit to look out the windshield with her da as they came to the first cabin of Grassy Narrows Reserve. Smoke from its chimney was caught in the pines.

Brian reached behind him to hug his daughter, supporting her to rest on his shoulder as he spoke to his wife. "Once I asked Joe Loon if he'd like to visit Ireland with me. He said he enjoyed my stories about it so much he saw no need."

"He'd rather see what you've put in his head?"

"Somethin' like that I guess, yeah."

"I wonder what that looks like, the Ireland he's created in his imagination."

"I have imagined bringin', say, Albert to Cong an' then getting' to listen, yeah, as he would describe what he saw to the others. Have you talked to Mary about goin'?"

"I just thought of it."

There were three more cabins in sight, covered in the snow, and more smoke indicated more cabins were just back in the trees.

Grace O'Malley was restless. "When am I going to see Little Stevie?"

Brian rubbed the back of her head. "Just hang on, Gracie girl, we're almost there."

"Or maybe Bri, what about this. Maybe Mary an' your Gracie girl should go with you to Chicago, an' then it makes all the sense for us to buy the Otter, yeah, so Dutch can fly all of you around."

The sound of the Bombardier approaching had drawn Albert and Old George from their cabins to walk down to the shoreline to greet their arrival. They waved to Brian and signaled the place they selected for him to bring the Bombardier up onto shore, then onto the road that cut through the trees. Brian stopped so they could climb in and Grace O'Malley asked where Little Stevie was and Albert gave directions to the cluster of cabins where many of Joe Loon's clan spent the winter.

The night sky was filled with so many bright stars that the Path of Souls was marked by a great streak of solid white starlight. The night was still and cold; the air seemed frozen. The people of Joe Loon's clan and others—Sturgeon, Crane, and Bear clans were represented—were bundled in their warmest coats and hats and boots and blankets, gathered around the large fire circle where a great blaze was tended by two teenage boys and an elder.

Smaller fires dotted the perimeter.

Among the many joyously celebrating were Joe Loon and Naomi and Simon, Mary Fobister and Little Stevie, Albert and his wife and their daughter and son, Old George, Mathew Beaver and his wife and children, Louis Angeconeb and his wife and children, and the Burkes; the other clans were of similar size, and over fifty people were gathered, celebrating.

The drummers beat their drums, and the singers chanted thanks and prayers to the Great Creator for all his many gifts. Many added thanks for sending them His son, Jesus the Christ.

They danced to give praise and they danced to keep warm, and This Man danced with them, his great buffalo robe draped over his shoulders.

A few quietly shared a bottle. After a sip, another joined the dance.

They continued for much of an hour, the drums and the chants in a cycle of thankful praise, smoke from the fires rising to vanish in the night, the fog of their breath rising with it, the spirits joined, the Ancestors dancing above.

When the drumming and singing stopped, a teenage girl from the Sturgeon clan took her sister by the hand, then Little Stevie took her other hand and Grace took his as the teenage girl invited all the children to join her. She shaped them into a choir, and they sang *Silent Night*, in the forest language.

Grace knew the first lines.

"Gichitwaa-dibikad, waaseyaaziwin maa, ayaamagad ayaad Mary, baanizid Abinoojii niigid, Christ sa gii-niigid."

Christmas afternoon offered a blue-sky dome for the bright white world. At the eastern edge of the last cluster of cabins was a clearing, and on the other side of the clearing a great thicket of bushy blue dogwood grew along the base of a sharp incline. In the summer the dogwood leaves formed a tight canopy that crowned at thirty feet. Even naked the dogwood branches were such an interwoven mass that every winter a good-sized snowdrift formed up against it and around it—the bushy trees and slope caught the wind and its snow; the smallest trees at the edge were scaffolding and a platform. This winter there had been two very heavy snowfalls by Christmas, and the winds blew just right, so there were many drifts and the largest was bigger than anyone remembered, nearly twenty feet tall and thirty feet deep for much of its over two hundred foot length.

For days the boys and girls had been digging and shaping a growing complex of tunnels and caves in the massive drift. Nearly a dozen children worked on new construction or played in what had already been built, when Little Stevie showed Grace O'Malley the tunnel he helped build. Maureen and Mary stood close by as their children crawled into the mouth of a tunnel, then deep into the snowdrift and out of sight.

Grace O'Malley went first, on her hands and knees, but after traveling six or seven feet in she stopped and rolled over on her back and took off her mitten so she could use her finger to engrave the image of a moose in the snow wall above her. Little Stevie watched and waited. She finished, put her mitten back on, and on all fours she covered the ten more feet of tunnel to find it ended as a small cavity in the snow, just big enough for the two of them, the trunk and branches of a dogwood showing through. They squeezed in together, their legs folded knees to chins. They wiggled their backs against the snow wall and looked back at the silver light in the tunnel; Little Stevie began to sing.

Maureen was on her knees leaning over to peer down the tunnel. She couldn't see the children but could hear the singing. It was *Silent Night*, in English.

Behind the two women, still back among the cabins and the trees, Brian and Joe Loon, Albert, Simon, and two other young men were headed their way. Albert told Brian that they were talking about trapping, so no useful purpose was served in translating for him, though he did share the occasional observation whenever they mentioned the portion of the River fished by the guests of The Great Lodge at Innish Cove.

Joe Loon was listening to the others talking about their trapping, but was thinking about the best time to look for the big beaver that had lived on the River's bank now flooded by the dam.

"When the ceremony of the Christ baby's birth is complete I will trap along Three Kill Creek. When I return it will be time to go to the new lake the white man has created. There is a secret there that will show us where the big beaver have gone."

Simon walked ahead of Joe Loon, to break the snow for him. He called back over his shoulder, "I will go with you Grandfather."

"We will wait for the marten moon as well so we can trap them along the ridges."

"I will be ready."

❄ ❄ ❄

Little Stevie was still singing, when Grace O'Malley, bored, and she led him back out of the tunnel. After their mothers rearranged their scarves and hats for them, Little Stevie showed Grace the entrance of a much longer tunnel. "Louie and Tall George, they built it. Others helped them. I helped them. But Louie and Tall George, they built it. They say it is the longest tunnel."

He led the way as the tunnel first went straight into the deepest and tallest portion of the snowdrift then offered tunnels left and right, down the center of the drift.

Little Stevie turned left.

Grace O'Malley turned right.

When Little Stevie realized Grace had not followed him, he turned to follow her. She led the way for ten yards or more and then the tunnel opened up to the grand cavern of the tunnel system, one large enough for ten children, though Grace found only Louie and Tall George. The two boys could stand in the center of the cavern, where the ceiling was highest, and Tall George was at work carving out more space from the ceiling; Louie was on his knees, patting the walls, compacting the snow against and into the dogwood branches, making the walls sturdier. They both turned when Grace entered and smiled with pride when they saw the look of wonder on her face.

She was amazed. She sat in the middle of the room and then Little Stevie sat next to her, and they were both amazed. The light shimmered silver blue. The domed space carved from the drift made her peaceful but the longer she sat there the more joyful she became, and she giggled and got up to dance about the room.

Maureen and Mary stood at the opening of the long tunnel. So many children climbed in and out of one hole then another that Maureen, still learning the physics of big snow, began to accept it as safe and focused on Mary.

"So if you're askin' me, an' assumin' you're interested at all, yeah, I think what's best for you an' what's best for the children an' what's best for me is all one in the same, an' that's for you an' the children to go with Bri an' Dutch to the States. I think some good would come of Little Stevie visitin' the cities where so many of our guests come from, yeah. An' it gives the children their best care, you an' Bri' lookin' after 'em rather than you an' family we pretend she knows. An' then there's this, that Bri's trip is six or seven days an' I'm near certain mine will take twice that long."

"I have never been away from my people for more than two days."

"That's why I said I won't be tryin' to convince you, it's only goin' to happen if you feel like takin' an adventure an' seein' some part of the world that you've not known."

"I would like to help you Sister. I will talk with Naomi tonight."

"Thanks for even considerin' it."

"You would have to lend me one of your traveling luggages or baggages."

"I figured we'd be buying you an' Little Stevie what you'd be needin' along with some travelin' clothes, if you'd like." Maureen switched to Ojibway to add, "To say thank you Sister."

When Maureen saw Brian approaching she left Mary to meet him half way and he stepped away from the men's conversation about trapping.

"She's agreed to talk about it with Naomi tonight, about goin' with you an' the children an' Dutch to Chicago."

"We need to know soon so we can finish our arrangements to use the Otter."

"Come see what the children have made. Grace has been explorin'."

At that moment Mary called out in alarm and Brian and Maureen saw the other men running the last distance to the big snowdrift. Brian pounded through deep snow and Maureen took his wake. Teenage boys tossed aside their toboggans, and Mary, and then Albert, joined the boys. The long length of the drift had caved in.

Mary called the children's names, and Maureen pleaded, "What is it?" Albert answered as he dug. "The drift collapsed. The children are buried."

But they could hear the children calling and their voices were strong as they expressed their alarm, and so they still moved quickly but their panic subsided. They could hear Grace O'Malley calling out that she was fine. They heard Little Stevie. Tommy Land was one of the tobogganers who dug where he heard his younger brother, Louie, who with Tall George was furiously digging up from the caved-in cavern. They met each other; Tommy pulled, Louie stood, and they tumbled out of the drift, followed by Tall George, as Brian, and then Maureen, arrived.

Grace and Little Stevie's voices had seemed to be right on top of each other, and when Albert dug away the next big armfuls of snow, he revealed the back of Little Stevie's coat.

"We've got them."

They dug away more snow and found Little Stevie had positioned himself as a barrier over Grace. He was on his hands and knees, and Grace's head and torso were under his protection.

❋ ❋ ❋

Later that night Brian took a lantern from Joe Loon's cabin where a pallet had been made for him and Maureen to spend the night. He left Maureen in conversation with the clan Elder and followed the path through the trees to Mary Fobister's cabin. Grace O'Malley had her pallet there, as an expansion of Little Stevie's bed, so they could spend all of her stay together. Brian was coming to check on his daughter and to thank Little Stevie again for protecting their Grace girl and to tell him, again, that he was the best big brother Grace could ever hope for.

But Mary greeted Brian with the news that Old George had visited the cabins and collected the children of Grassy Narrows to bring them to his cabin. She told him where to find it.

When Brian arrived, Old George was surrounded by children and sitting on a stump next to the wood burning stove. The one room cabin was filled with the children. He realized Old George had been in the middle of telling them a story when he saw how his arrival disrupted it all. The children didn't turn until Old George's look condemned the visitor, and he told Brian to sit in the corner or leave; when Old George realized his command had been in the forest language, the language of storytelling, he repeated it in English, but Brian had figured out what he meant. He found a corner out of the children's way and sat down on the floor, wishing immediately he was closer to the stove; he settled in, and wrapped himself tight.

Grace O'Malley was sitting at Old George's feet, next to Little Stevie. When she looked up and saw the visitor was her da she was able to navigate the room so easily that Little Stevie didn't realize she'd gone, Old George wasn't aware of her movement, and Brian was surprised when she dropped to nestle into his lap.

Old George returned to the ancient legend he was telling the children. It was a story he could tell only on a winter night when the ground was frozen. It was on a Christmas night six years earlier that Old George told this story of an orphan boy named New Star and his journey to find the greatest chief of all the people. It had become a new tradition, for him to gather all the children and tell them this story every Christmas night.

He took a small step back into the story, and began again; Grace was learning the native tongue and understood some words and a few phrases; Brian had no understanding but loved the sound of it.

Grace and her father enjoyed being so close to each other and so close to the room's magic.

"Long, long ago, tall dark storm clouds filled the sky. It began to rain. It rained day after day, day after day, until the earth was flooded. First the tallest trees were covered by the floodwaters. Then the tallest mountains were covered by the floodwaters. When the waters rose so high, all of the Original People that Great Creator had created were drowned. All of the animals that lived on the land were drowned. Only the creatures who could live in the water survived the terrible flood.

"Many moons passed and the land was flooded. Sky Woman looked down on the great flood. She was so sad, for she missed the earth and all of its creatures. She was very lonely. That is when Great Sea Turtle who is the father of all turtles rose to the surface of the flood waters, for he did not like seeing Sky Woman so sad and lonely. That is when Great Sea Turtle called out to Sky Woman.

Great Sea Turtle invited her to come down to rebuild the earth on the back of his great big shell.

"It brought Sky Woman great happiness to accept this invitation from Great Sea Turtle—"

Grace O'Malley reached up to pull her da's head close for her whisper. "Old George is telling a story about a lot of rain. And about a turtle."

"—She sent word to all the water animals that survived the flood asking for their help. When they gathered around she asked them to fetch her some mud from the bottom of the deep flood waters for she needed this mud to rebuild earth on the back of Great Sea Turtle's shell.

"All of the animals that heard her call came to help her. First Otter dove into the deep floodwaters. Otter was under water for a very long time, but when he surfaced he was out of breath. He failed to find the bottom."

Again Grace O'Malley whispered. "Nigig is Otter."

"Then it was Beaver's turn to try. He dove down deep into the water. He swam deeper than he had ever gone before. But he could not find the bottom, so Beaver had to return to the surface of the water exhausted.

"Then Loon tried. She called out and then slipped into the water. She dove deeper and deeper, but it got too dark and too cold for her to continue her search so she returned without any mud for Sky Woman.

"That is when Muskrat offered to try. All the other animals laughed at him, for they knew little Muskrat was not as strong as they were.

"Muskrat pretended he didn't hear their laughter, and he dove into the floodwaters. He swam deep into the cold and dark water, deeper and deeper he went. He was down there a long long time. Muskrat was down there so long that the other animals stopped laughing. He was down there so long the other animals became afraid for he was underwater much longer than any of them had been.

"Sky Woman and the other animals were just giving up hope when Muskrat's body rose to the surface and floated there in the water, as still as death. All of the animals gathered around Muskrat. They watched as Sky Woman breathed life into Muskrat. That is when it was discovered that Muskrat had found the bottom of the deep, deep floodwaters, for there was a small bit of mud in his paws.

"Sky Woman used this mud to rebuild the earth on Great Sea Turtle's shell. And to show her thanks Sky Woman gave all turtles the gift of understanding the speech of all Great Creator's creatures. And that is why all Ojibway and our brothers of the Three Fires call this place Turtle Island."

When Brian checked, he found his daughter was fast asleep, a smile on her lips.

Chapter 6

DEPARTURES AND ARRIVALS

THE BURKES LIVED in a modest townhouse in Kenora. It was the night before Brian and Grace O'Malley would leave it for the fishing shows in Chicago. Brian was in the bedroom finishing his packing while Maureen checked to make sure Grace was sleeping. Brian and Maureen had begun sipping before supper—the Irish for him, wine for her—and each had kept a glass close by throughout the evening, so they would be fueled just right by the flirting it brought on, teased and tuned just right for the late night love making Maureen still called their heroic fuck, the sort of sex they always attempted to mark a departure or return, to celebrate a success or the anniversary of one.

Most often they did accomplish some version of what they wanted to achieve; delighted at the start and carried away by all their many variations of energetic going in and coming out and then the long sprint of the back stretch, each of them lost to all but the both of them together at the great convergence then emergence of bliss.

Brian put on his robe and shuffled in the dark to the bathroom down the hall, then headed to the living room bar for one last nip. When he returned to bed, Maureen had lit two candles, for Grace had climbed into their bed and was already sleeping curled next to her mother. He looked down at them in the soft light.

"Our Grace has your grace."

"Fueled by your fire."

Brian settled into bed next to them.

"Since you know our itinerary an' we won't know yours, it's you who has to call us, an' regularly."

"I will."

He gently took her arm.

"Regularly."

"I will."

"Frequently an' regularly."

"I will."

"If the IRA don't blow up all the telephone lines with their next god damned—"

"It's a smart move their part, effective, an' no casualties."

"A smart move? A smart move? When someone figures out a great way to rob a bank, you gonna credit thugs with makin' smart moves?"

"You promised me, Bri."

"I'm sorry. Yes, I promised you. I'm angry that's all."

"Angry? How can you be angry after what we just did wit' each other an' with our Gracie girl lyin' between us?"

"I'm still angry you ain't comin' to Chicago."

"Well take care, because when you call them thugs then I have to say, 'So if they're thugs, what's the proper label for what the Brits are?' an' then we're off on an all-night argument again."

Brian took her in his arms.

"I said I'm sorry. It's just that I'm scared, Lady Girl. I don't want you anywhere 'round Derry, an' I'm angry at anyone an' everythin' that threatens ya, so."

"The IRA threat is aimed at the illegal forces of British occupation, not the Irish. Not the true Irish."

Brian pulled the covers up over their daughter.

"When Grace O'Malley Burke was born in a wigwam this place became her home. She's Canadian. An' she's rooted me so deep here I don't even think about all that drama anymore."

"You got children there as well."

"Livin' free in Dublin an' Cong, an' inclined to think about me only when I ask them to… An' for good or for ill they don't care so much about the Six Counties neither, not like we all did once upon a time."

"Just so, you respect I still do an' will 'til the Brits are gone."

"Go get your mum an' bring her home with you an' maybe you'll find you can care a bit less."

"I'll bring her back if she'll come, but what you're askin' me to do beyond that, I hear it as forgettin' those heroes who died for—"

Brian held her tight to his big chest, just the way she liked it.

"I said I was sorry."

"I'll be thinkin' of this moment the whole time."

"Just come back to us as soon as you can."

They were at the Kenora Airport, loading luggage into the brand new de Havilland Otter rented to them for the trip. The plane was bright red, with gold trim, the interior set up with plush seats, a more deluxe package than the bush plane NOA was buying. Maureen settled Grace into her seat next to Little Stevie, behind the pilot and co-pilot's chairs, and in front of Mary. Maureen was strapping a seat belt around her daughter and tucking picture books close at hand, and barely holding back her tears.

"You an' Little Stevie will have a grand adventure."

Grace O'Malley reached against the constraints of the seat belt to hug her mother.

"I want you to come."

Maureen had hugged her daughter all morning; they were parting for the first time, and this last hug released the first tears that she'd been fighting since dawn.

"Da is with you—" The deep sadness in her voice surprised her. She leaned back to include Mary with her comment.

"—and if ever ya need Mary to be your Mum, she'll hold you in her arms."

"Azhegiiwe. Until your mother returns."

Brian was settling into the co-pilot's chair and Maureen turned to him for respite. She wiped the tears before she leaned forward with her elbows on the back of each chair, then rested the side of her head on Brian's for a moment before she stood as tall as the ceiling allowed.

"I picture Mary an' the children at the hotel an' you showin'

Dutch the blues joints."

"An' Greek town."

"Make sure he takes you to Halsted Street, Dutch."

"Make you wish you were comin' with us?"

"Actually, it does."

"There's an empty seat back there, an' you're already packed."

She cut him off with a kiss, hugged each of them one last time, and then left, slamming the fuselage door shut and checking twice that it was closed tight.

Dutch taxied to position to await his clearance. The snow was packed high along all the runways, the wind was gusting, it was bitterly cold, but Maureen stayed outside on the hanger apron where they had loaded the Otter, and watched the plane take the runway, set itself, then accelerate into a smooth take off. As soon as the plane was safely up and away, she left, shivering.

That afternoon Maureen returned to the airport to take the commercial flight to Winnipeg to make her connection to New York, to fly to Dublin, where she planned to hire a car for the trip to the North, to Derry, to call on her mother.

And to see Kevin.

Joe Loon and Simon were bundled with layers and their warmest coats for the coldest weather, for nights below zero and days below freezing. Around their necks and tucked under their layers they wore their magic in small leather pouches. Simon broke the way in the deep snow for Joe Loon as they snowshoed single file through the trees. Joe Loon had the clan's rifle strapped to his pack. Simon had a small killing club hanging from his rope belt. Their traps hung from slings across their shoulders, down their backs, and from their waists.

They followed Joe Loon's trap line as it ran up from the River along a feeder stream. After Mathew Loon was shot they named it Three Kill Creek, when someone recalled that the winter before he died Mathew Loon caught a beaver in each of his first three traps the first day he set them. They set four traps, sized and placed for beaver.

So far north in winter the useful day was short and they worked it steadily so they could be back at their cabin by nightfall. The next day, at first sun, they would walk the trap line again, checking for success.

The Otter's approach to Chicago took them along the shore of Lake Michigan. When they saw the city rising on the horizon Brian called the children to come sit in his lap so he could tell them stories of the amazing castles the people of Chicago have built.

"The first people to live here were brothers to the Ojibway called the Potawatomie. They named this place Chee Kwa Gwa."

As they flew along the lakeshore approaching the great cityscape, Brian pointed out the Wrigley Building and Tribune Tower. Brian and Maureen had visited the Tribune Tower during one of their previous trips, and he told Dutch what he remembered.

"When it was built they gathered stones from historic places 'round the world, an' used them in the buildin' of it. They've used stone from the Great Wall of China, from the Coliseum in Rome, from the Cathedral at Notre Dame, places of that sort, yeah. I guess they figured sacred stone would glorify their office buildin'."

"It looks to be a pretty glorious office building."

"One thing I've learned running our camp, you can always count on Americans bein' American."

"That's a comforting thought, actually."

"I guess it is."

"What about the Irish?"

"The Irish?"

"Can you count on the Irish always being Irish—yes, this is Canadian Registry CA two two four, approaching at…"

Before Maureen left the Dublin Airport in her rented car, she called the shop nearest her mother's cottage with a telephone, a shop that took messages delivered by the shop lad, and word was sent that Maureen had arrived and was on her way.

But first, she drove into the city, and parked on a street between

Kevin's store and his townhouse. She found the store closed and the townhouse empty. She found a telephone box and called the last Dublin number she had for Kevin, but no one answered.

She returned to her car and headed to the North, crossing the border into the Six Counties on the road from Dundalk to Newry, the road that headed to Portadown. When she arrived in Portadown she stopped at a public phone box and rang a local number. She had used this phone box for similar purposes years before.

After a few rings a man answered.

"Was a time I used this number to leave a message."

"Who's the message for?"

"Kevin."

"Kevin?"

"If I did so now, would he be gettin' it?"

"Perhaps."

"An' when might that be?"

"Tomorrow's even.'"

"Can't get it to him tonight?"

"Don't know I can get it to him t'all."

"But you will try."

"The message?"

"Lady Girl is visitin' Mum."

"Lady Girl is visiting Mum."

"For Kevin, yeah."

"So why is Lady Girl visiting Mum?"

"Thanks for your help."

Meigs Field was a single strip airport on a man-made, offshore island in Lake Michigan. Dutch obtained clearance and set the Otter down smoothly.

As they taxied in Brian patted Dutch's shoulder and thanked him for the great flight. Dutch smiled and said, "Airports on a constructed island today, Halstead Street blues later. That's Americans being American."

"Poetry, an' songs for martyrs of lost causes."

"What?"

"That's Irish being Irish."

✳ ✳ ✳

Maureen stopped again, in Omagh, and rang a second number. The man who answered told her to stay near the phone box; he'd ring her right back, for he thought he knew where Kevin was.

It was thirty minutes later before the phone rang; Maureen had just begun to wonder if she should leave.

"Kevin will meet Lady Girl at Lough Neagh, tomorrow. At the same place and time of day they met there before. He asks you to confirm Lady Girl will be there."

"Lough Neagh, tomorrow. At the same place an' time of day they met there before. Lady Girl will be there."

✳ ✳ ✳

It was late at night when Maureen pulled off the road that continued north to Derry, onto the side road that led to her family cottage. Her mother lived there alone now. They fixed a pot of tea, set out biscuits and a bit of cold meat. Maureen found the feel of her father was still there, and she was glad. His picture on the mantle; his pipes in the rack sat on the shelf; his smell was gone but a sense of how he stood in the room remained; and he was at the table with them while her mother spoke about family members.

When Maureen told stories about Grace O'Malley and her new friend, the famous American writer Ernest Hemingway, she found she was speaking to her mum and her da.

Maureen realized how exhausted she was, kissed her mother good night, and she curled up in the bed she had slept in as a child; she listened for the sounds her da had made as he puttered about the cottage at night, and she heard them.

✳ ✳ ✳

A car passed by her mother's cottage in the early morning, slowed a moment when the driver found what he was looking for—a hired car parked in the yard—and then it drove on.

✳ ✳ ✳

Joe Loon and Simon returned from Three Kill Creek with one beaver and their traps dangling and jangling. Joe Loon skinned the beaver and gave it to Naomi to prepare the meat for roasting. Then they checked their gear, and supplies, for they would leave again, the next day, to find the big beaver, and they would be in the winter forests for two or three days before they'd return.

※ ※ ※

It was just after dawn, in County Atrim, the sun still low over the North Channel and Rathland Island. Two men found each other just above the basalt columns of the Giants Causeway. One offered the other a cigarette and they turned their backs against the open water breezes to light up, cupped hands for two on a match.

"When I realized who it was asking after Kevin Coogan I told Trevor to keep checking the O'Toole cottage, to drive by and keep an eye on any happenings. He found her hired car there early this morning."

"Have you actually laid eyes on her?"

"Not yet."

"Do any of your fellas claim to have actually laid eyes on her?

"Not yet."

"Then you don't know if it's her car, and you don't even know if she's returned. I can't pass this on to Stormont until we're sure. The last of the London Bombers is what they call her, and this means too much to them for me to be wrong."

"I'm sure."

"I can't be sure until you've seen her."

"A bird calls an old IRA contact to say she's looking for Kevin and she says to tell him she's visiting her mum. That night a hired car from Dublin shows up at Donovan O'Toole's cottage. And you're not sure. I gotta say, what the feck."

"This is too important to them. They'll ask me if I have positive eye witness confirmation it's her, and right now you haven't given it to me."

"So you won't be paying me my money."

"You haven't earned it yet."

"My fellas, as you call them, is all of them expecting me to come back with the money."

"Sounds like you're disappointing the lot of us."

"You know Jerry, you were a bastard as a lad and it's sure nothing has changed."

"Ah ha, but don't I remember as a lad you being a feckin' Fenian and so now everything's changed with you turning on them."

"I haven't changed. It's the time that's changed. Any chance of driving the British out of here is long past. I realize it. They haven't."

Maureen stood behind her mother's cottage watching the sunrise. She turned when she heard her mother knocking about inside and went in. When she announced the trip she would be taking later in the day, to meet Kevin, she didn't mention anything about its purpose: to find her father's murderer.

"What makes you think Kevin's to be trusted?"

"Ah Mum, the day comes I can't trust Kevin, that's the day I'll never be able to stop lookin' over me shoulder."

"It's just the papers, they're full a stories of two or three groups all claimin' to be the true heirs to the Uprisin', the real IRA, the True Fenians and such. Seems they're fightin' each other as much as takin' on Brits."

"It's the Brits puttin' those sorts of stories out for you to read, yeah. They're masters at it, plantin' falsehoods to confuse you. They've even a name for it. *Disinformation* is what they call it."

"If so, then so, but you know yourself since the days of the Big Fellow an' Dev it has always been so. When men struggle for power sooner or later, *et tu Brute*; an' some are sayin' it's worse than ever it was before. So I do worry for your safety."

"If I could tell you the spot he chose to meet you'd feel better Mum, I'm sure you would; it's the safest of our old rendezvous. I'll be back for your birthday."

This Man was bundled in his thick buffalo robe, and his legs were wrapped in hides and furs. His snowshoes sunk in the new snow but carried him over the packed base. He walked along the shore of the River, at the sacred place where the fires burned for days, long before the white man called it Innish Cove.

Joe Loon and Simon left Grassy Narrows to find the big beaver.

Along with their supplies for three days and their beaver traps, they carried one foothold trap sized for marten, for the heavy forested ridges leading to the River's new lake were prime marten habitat.

In Chicago, the diner just off the hotel lobby was crowded with hunting and fishing camp owners and outfitters, from all over Ontario, from Minnesota and Wisconsin and the UP, and from a few western states as well. The fishing and hunting show filled the hotel's grand ballroom and two largest halls, and the men were enjoying their breakfasts; at one table they found further enjoyment when they slipped a shot of the good stuff in their coffee, then passed the bottle to their neighbors.

They wore buckskin vests or buckskin jackets, or moccasins or cowboy boots, or fishing vests or hunting shirts, or fishing caps or cowboy hats. The room was filled with hearty laughter, boastful stories, and enthusiastic greetings.

Brian and Dutch were planning the day; Mary was attending to the kids eating their hotcakes; they called them moon breads, for Simon told all the village children the story of the first time he and Mathew Loon, the River's true warrior, had eaten them. Brian would man the booth, and Dutch would take the others to spend the day at the Lincoln Park Zoo. They would meet back at the hotel coffee shop at six, get the children fed and settled in a room for the night with a babysitter the hotel was arranging, and then Brian would take Dutch and Mary to see Willie Smith and Big Boy Spires at the Halsted Street blues club he and Maureen had enjoyed so thoroughly the year before.

Chapter 7
WORLDS BETWEEN

MAUREEN WAS DRIVING through a soft rain, heading southeast on a lonely road that led through the wild moors of County Tyrone. A car had been following her since she had been on the road, well back, then out of sight before it re-appeared. She approached a crossroads and considered turning to see if the car followed, then decided to go straight through. She relaxed and even laughed at herself when the car behind her turned north at the crossroads.

She continued on the moor road on a course towards Toome, a village on the north shore of Lough Neagh. When another car appeared in her rear view mirror a few minutes later she did not know it had been following the first car, the one that turned off at the crossroads. The second car had followed the first at a measured distance, by plan, and she couldn't have suspected that the driver of the first car was headed to the nearest phone box to confirm he had seen Maureen with his own eyes and that the second car was still tailing her.

In the winter there were very few people at the zoo; Chicagoans knew most of the animals would be inside, either lying in a concrete box behind bars or pacing nervously behind thick glass or out of view entirely in back rooms, and when Dutch and Mary and the children realized this they found they were making their way quickly past anxiously pacing big cats and swaying and chained elephants but more and more empty cages, and the animals' captive appearance in the cold damp concrete behind heavy bars made them all feel empty.

Then they entered the Primate House, led by Grace O'Malley and Little Stevie, Dutch and Mary right behind them. There was more movement here, more life and sound. When the children saw the gorillas they ran to the cage, but as they drew close they slowed their pace and almost tiptoed the last distance. Mary picked up Grace O'Malley and Dutch picked up Little Stevie so they could stand on the rail and to get the closest view of the huge silver back male in the middle of the enclosure.

The gorilla sat on his haunches, the front of his massive torso open towards his admirers, but his head turned away, in profile, as he ate from the bushel of green stalks the attendant had tossed in his cage moments before. The children watched as the silver back held a stalk with his feet and one hand, and ripped strips with his teeth to chew them. Both children worked their lips in mimic of the gorilla.

Then the gorilla stopped chewing and turned his head to look full face to the children, and Grace O'Malley stared into his eyes, and Little Stevie stared into his eyes, and Dutch and Mary felt the children immediately and completely captivated.

They stood very still, very quiet, for as long as the gorilla looked their way, though Grace was slowly leaning forward as Mary held her back. Dutch was hardly needed for Little Stevie to maintain his easy balance on the rail. Even when the gorilla looked away the children remained still. When finally released from the spell, Grace O'Malley whispered to Little Stevie, "He is asking us why he is in there. He wants to know why we don't let him out."

It was barely a mist of rain. Kevin stood on the east end of the bridge that crossed the River at Toome when Maureen drove across from the west. She saw him, pulled the car to the side of the road, and walked his way. Kevin smiled at the sight of her.

"You remembered."

"Do I remember the first thing you taught, the last thing you taught, an' everythin' between, yes I do. The very first thing you taught was a meetin' in Dungannon designates a meetin' at Toome Bridge."

"We met here when you started training for London operations."

The hug they shared when they met at the foot of the bridge was quick but genuine. Maureen pulled away first.

"You found the fellow that murdered me da?"

"That's why you came?"

She found she couldn't answer that at first. She looked past Kevin at the River rushing by. "I told Brian I've come to bring me Mum back to Kenora." She turned her back and paused. "I've wondered if I've come to help you." She faced Kevin again. "But I need to know right now, Kevin, have you found the bastard?"

"We have identified him."

"An' you're certain he's the murderer?"

"We know it was him."

"Show him to me an' I'll tell you for dead certain. I'll never forget the bastard's face."

"We found him. But we haven't been watching him so close that we know for sure where he is at this moment."

Maureen reached in her coat pocket.

"So you were lurin' me with a false promise?"

"You sent neither word nor sign of any sort that you wanted us to keep him in our sights for you. We do have other matters that need attending, as you well know."

She pulled out the newspaper clipping.

"But you said you found him."

She unfolded the newspaper and showed the clear message to Kevin.

"This was in your second envelope."

"When I sent it, we knew where he was. When I got the word you were here, I asked about and I have good information that will help us locate him again. Now that you're back."

Maureen looked away.

"Who knows we're meetin'?"

"No one."

Maureen walked to the other side of the bridge and Kevin spoke to her back as he followed her.

"I'm meeting tonight with the lad who has been tracking him down. He's been on it a day but the trail was fresh. He'll know where he is."

Maureen leaned on the rail, watching the River's eddies and currents, and Kevin stood with her. She turned to take in the bridge.

"Da's song—one he loved to sing—it's set right here, yeah."

"It was set at the old bridge." Kevin recited with a sing-song rhythm. "Oh Ireland, Mother Ireland, you love them still the best, the fearless brave who fighting fall upon your hapless breast, but ne'er a one of all your dead more bravely fell in fray, as Roddy McCorley goes to die on the bridge of Toome today."

"He left the fight, twice."

"That's right. He stayed away from it for nearly a year, hiding out up in the mountains, before he came back. When he went to Derry, intending to migrate to America, he knew he couldn't go, that he was needed here."

"I was thinkin' of Da. He left twice as well... but since he never got out of Derry either time, well, maybe he never left at all."

"The both of them, Donovan O'Toole and McCorley, they kept coming back because they knew how crucial a role they played for a cause that grows more noble with each sacrifice."

"You wrote something like that in your second letter."

"Each year that the Brits keep what they stole, they make a greater tear in the fabric of justice. Each time another martyr is slain, they stain that fabric with their blood. It becomes a higher calling, each year, to repair it, to cleanse it. To restore justice."

"An' here's where we all nod an' agree physical force is all the Brits understand."

"Nothing else has ever worked. I don't need to tell Maureen O'Toole that."

Maureen turned toward town.

"You told me the gallows where they hung McCorley were there." She pointed to a spot above the River bank next to a maple tree. "But I've had others insist it was the other side of town, behind the police barracks." She turned back to Kevin. "You know what else McCorley and Da had in common?"

"Of course I do."

"Both of them betrayed to the Brits by native sons—both of them."

"After McCorley was hanged, the Brits disemboweled him. They were no more civilized with your da, forcing his family to watch as they put a bullet in his head."

Kevin stood at Maureen's side, put his arm around her shoulders, and held her gently.

"When first we met here, Da's Fenian songs, they sounded like battle cries to my ear, yeah. They were glorious."

"And now?"

"Now? Now I can hear the threat of the gallows more plainly."

They were quiet. The River rolled along. The rain stopped. A vehicle approached the bridge and drove past. It was the second tail car. When it crossed the bridge the driver turned right and stopped just out of sight.

Kevin turned to look Maureen full in the face. "I'll make it plain and simple for you. We drive them out of the North right now. Or it's never."

Maureen pulled a step away.

"You said now or never in the letter you sent a year ago."

"When we had our best chance but too many of our finest sat out as the campaign began. Now we're a year into it, and the job is more difficult today but no less…"

"Noble?"

"If we miss this last chance… Maureen, we'll be accepting the Brits get to keep what they took from us, now and forever, and that all those who gave their lives trying to re-unite it died without purpose."

"You said all that in your second letter."

"What, it sounds so grotesquely Irish from across the ocean that you allow yourself to mock these truths? It doesn't make them less true. And if you agree with that observation, then you have to follow any course of action to find justice, or you betray justice."

"So say you."

"Donovan O'Toole's daughter knows the truth in all I'm saying."

Maureen turned to the rail and studied the town along the bank. She was quiet. Kevin stood next to her, waiting for her to speak.

"Maureen O'Toole Burke."

"What."

"You called me Maureen O'Toole. I am Maureen O'Toole *Burke*."

"But the O'Toole is still there, right in the middle of you."

Again she was quiet, watching a small piece of wood caught in a back flow current, spinning about. A voice echoed down the street.

"You say you have other matters that demand your attention. You're planning a new operation."

"We have targets under consideration and I've got us a team."

"But no plan."

"Targets and the team."

Maureen looked up at Kevin.

"I have a daughter now."

"Living peacefully in an Eden paid for by IRA money."

"No. A trusted friend can't be sayin' that. I paid it back, in arms. We all agreed... If I find I am here to help the Cause, it must accept my loyalty to it... Now an' forever, yeah."

"Sorry... I'm sorry. But tell me how you expect you'll discover why you're here and what you're going to do?"

"I'll listen."

"You could meet them now, our team, if you wanted to, to find out about your da's murderer and see we'd have a good—"

She turned on him as he sparked her guilt to flash to anger.

"Don't call it *our* team."

"They'll all be gathering this evening. You could meet them."

"You told them about me being here?"

"I've not made mention of you to anyone. Not even the fellow who called you back knows who he called."

"I called the old number in Portadown first."

"They're still with us." Kevin was surprised to find he didn't feel as confident about that as he tried to sound. He'd have to check into that. "So come spend the evening and we'll discover something in Donovan O'Toole's memory so inspired, it tips the balance."

"Where?"

"You know I love you Lady Girl, but I couldn't tell you. You'd have to come with me."

"You know the fellow will be there, who can lead us to Da's murderer?"

"I know he will be there."

"Let me get a message to Mum first."

"There's a phone box around the corner."

Joe Loon and Simon walked and worked all day, following the patterns and paths and traces of their prey, setting traps with enticements of bait in places the marten wanted to go. They spoke very little as they made their way through the hard, cold, and deep snow.

Joe Loon and Simon walked and worked all day, following the patterns and paths and traces of their prey, setting traps with enticements of bait in places the marten wanted to go. They spoke very little as they made their way through the hard, cold, and deep snow.

This Man made his way from the shore up the slight slope to the grove of young birch trees. He stood in front of the trees and looked back over the frozen cove and River, and he called to the spirits of the men and women and children who had died from the white man pox and who were burned in the fires. The remnants of the funeral pyres that had blazed day after day years ago could still be seen, tips of the last charred logs sticking out above the snow.

His call was captured in a song cycle that he repeated, over and over, announcing to the spirits that they were needed.

Kevin led Maureen to his car and they drove out to the main street, heading southeast on the Belfast road.

The driver of the car who had followed Maureen to Toome watched from his vantage point, dashed down the sidewalk to round the corner to see which road they chose, then ran back to his car and headed out in the same direction.

Kevin and Maureen drove along the north shore of Lough Neagh. The road hugged the shore, dipping south then heading north as they approached Antrim Bay.

"So you've read both letters. Did you read the articles and policy papers?"

"I did."

"The Americans handled their end getting the packages

delivered to you?"

"The fellow you sent from Boston was a proper lad. I didn't like your Chicago boyos."

"We heard what you did to them. Turning fishes into revolvers."

"I wasn't sure who I was sending a message to, actually. A big part of it was me tellin' you to let me be."

"And still, you came."

"I've always wondered what I'd do if you found the man who shot Da."

They drove in quiet.

"Tell me it's Antrim town we're headed for an' not Belfast."

"It's Antrim."

"Ten minutes."

"Fifteen."

"Then here's how I see my smartest move for now—"

She told him her terms for attending the meeting, he accepted. Kevin shared details of recent operations, mostly failed, as they drove the rest of the way. The car approached then entered Antrim and turned off the main road on a quiet street of townhouses; Maureen nodded when Kevin identified the townhouse where they would meet as he drove past it to park around a corner. Kevin got out of the car, but Maureen waited five minutes before she took a round and about route to the townhouse.

The tailing car passed the side street just as Kevin entered the townhouse and the driver got a quick glimpse of him. He doubled back, parked, and found a good vantage point by the time Maureen knocked on the door and Kevin let her in.

Maureen joined Kevin in the parlor; they planned to get there before the others arrived. Maureen looked around the room.

"Have you met here before?"

"Not recently."

There were stairs to the second floor.

"Any reason for anyone to go upstairs?"

"No, but you might prefer this, is what I'm thinking."

Kevin pushed aside the high back chair that blocked a view of a half size door leading to a small closet under the stairs.

"I could leave the door open a little, put the chair back where it was. You're in the room without anyone knowing it."

Maureen smiled. "You remember Joe Loon?"

"Of course."

"Then you remember he doesn't speak English an' understands little. He tells Brian what he learns about who a white man is mostly comes from listenin' to what sort a sound he makes, what his voice sounds like when he is surprised, or when he is callin' out to his friends. Oh, an' especially when all day long his friend is catchin' fish an' he isn't, Joe Loon tells us that what the voice sounds like at the end of that day tells him everythin' worth knowin' about a man."

"Well, get comfortable in there, for a number of these are the sorts that like the sounds they're making with their voices."

As the long dusk approached early night fall, Joe Loon and Simon arrived at the small snow covered wigwam that Joe Loon's father built with his father in the old times when he first trapped this watershed forest—someone from the clan visited it almost every summer to make sure it was ready for a winter visit, and over the years the repairs had nearly rebuilt the structure. They dug the snow from the wigwam door and piled it around the outside of the shelter to help keep them warm inside; they collected firewood, and then they settled in for the long winter night.

Simon started a small fire in the wigwam's fire pit while Joe Loon set out some of the food Naomi packed for them.

From out of the dark shadows Trapper leaned forward, enjoying the fire's warmth.

Before they ate, Joe Loon thanked the spirits of this place, then the spirit of Marten, then the spirit of Beaver. He asked the spirit of Beaver to recognize him, to know him as the man who never takes too many of the big beaver wherever he finds them, and to guide him the next morning when they continue on to the new lake that hides the shore of the River.

He reminded the spirit of Beaver that their ancestors had lived together since the earliest of days. He told the spirit of Beaver that for the old ways to continue they must continue to live the old ways, and that he was there to stay true to them. Then he thanked the ancestors, and they ate.

Later, as they slept, Trapper was still praying, to the spirit of Beaver.

✳ ✳ ✳

Maureen took a pillow from the couch, pen and paper from the desk, and settled into a corner of the tight closet a few minutes before Kevin expected the first man to arrive. When the man arrived Kevin invited him to sit in the chair in front of the closet door. His voice sounded familiar to Maureen as he talked with Kevin about a hurling match he recently attended. The next two men offered strangers' voices and the topic was still hurling, though a different match.

The fourth voice, again a new one to Maureen's ear, brought an elaborate and long-winded story about an arrest of one of their men. Maureen didn't know any of the names he mentioned as he told his story, and it was hard for her to determine the significance of it, for the man telling the story found it quite important, but the others decidedly less so, or perhaps they had grown bored as the telling of it dragged on and on, with every small detail shared, then revisited.

She hoped to hear Kevin asking about her da, but what followed were generally confused voices as two men introduced a recent rumor of infiltration that others outside this group had shared with them, and now all of them seemed determined to interpret each statement twice, to reexamine each fact again and again. The familiar voice, the one close at hand, muttered something to someone; Maureen couldn't make it out, but someone laughed, and she grew more anxious at the absence of any reference to the search for the murderer of Donovan O'Toole.

The next topic for discussion began with a well-organized sound to it, bringing her some renewed hope. One voice reviewed the inventory of mines and other explosives. A second voice read an inventory of their cache of machine guns—Stens and Brens and grease guns—as well as M1s and hand guns, and ammunition, acknowledging that the Ebrington Barracks raid, the raid Maureen had led, was still the source of most of the arms. No one mentioned her by name when they talked about the raid, and that pleased her, but she felt a surge of deep pride and her memories of the thrill of it made her smile.

The armament reports triggered debates, first a quick and slightly humorous one about the relative merits of Sten and grease machine guns, then a longer one about whether the cache of weapons should be divided into smaller lots and dispersed, and finally an anxious one about how they might handle the problems another unit had recently when a mine exploded unexpectedly, maiming a unit member.

Then Maureen was deeply disheartened to hear the voices speak of a hurling match coming up in the next few days, and after a little bit of that the familiar voice in the chair excused himself, then one by one the others said goodbye, until Kevin told Maureen she could come out.

There was nothing said about her da, and as Kevin collapsed back in his chair she stood before him with a condemning look.

"You never took the risk of meetin' unless it was of vital importance. What was that?"

"Proof."

"Proof of what?"

"Of how badly I need your help, Lady Girl. Right now."

"Why didn't you ask about me da?"

"The fellow finding him for us wasn't here. He was supposed to come, I don't…"

Maureen walked into the kitchen to get a glass of water for Kevin. She had seen him tired before, but never like this; this reminded her of when she had met Sean Russell, in Berlin, when he had failed in his efforts to recruit the Nazis for a joint invasion of Northern Ireland. These two men weren't just tired—they were worn down and worn out.

She was confused about her feelings. She was eager to discover the location of her da's murderer so she could find out what she would do, and so she was disappointed the fellow with the information didn't come; those reactions didn't surprise her. What she hadn't expected was the feeling that took over during the discussion of the Ebrington Barracks raid, the feelings of pride and satisfaction that lingered on. She was angry at Kevin for being so ineffective, and then she was sorry to see Kevin slouched in the chair, his head back, his legs stretched out into the room, looking so fully deflated if not defeated. He took the glass of water from her and drank deeply.

"So how do I contact your man?"

Kevin was quiet. She sat down across from him.

"Tell me all you know about your man and what he's learned."

She unfolded her sheet of paper and sat on the couch across from Kevin. As he began to share what he knew, and she took notes, there was a knock on the door.

This Man continued his song cycle at the birch grove as winter followed winter, as all traces of the pyres burnt logs vanished, and as the birch trees seeded more trees that matured and died and fed the new growth with their own decay.

Maureen returned to the closet under the stairs and then Kevin answered the door. Her heart was pounding. She heard him greet the new arrival and hoped that sounds of them sitting down together meant this was the man they were waiting for. Her heart raced faster when she heard his pronouncement.

"I found him where he was so I'm—"

When the closest door suddenly swung open the man reached for his pistol hidden in his coat pocket. Kevin stood to assure him.

"No, no, you won't be needing that."

The man looked from Maureen to Kevin to Maureen again, and smiled with a respectful nod.

"You're Maureen O'Toole?"

"That's right."

"I know where to find the man who murdered your da."

"I need you to take me there."

He sat back down.

"You need to take me there now."

Kevin sat down. "Let's listen to what he has to say."

The man explained that the fellow was no longer a Black and Tan, but had joined the Royal Ulster Constabulary, he was an officer in the regular police force, and was still stationed in Banbridge, where he first located him two years before.

"His name is—"

"Wait." She thought for a moment. "I don't want to know his name."

"Tell her everything else you know about him."

It wasn't very much beyond that, that he'd been stationed in Banbridge for two years. And they found him as a happenstance; he needed to tell the tale whenever he was well into the whiskey and one night a true Irish patriot undercover heard him brag about being the triggerman, the man who executed the Fenian bastard Donovan O'Toole.

They talked well into the night until Kevin declared it was time for them to find beds, for they had an important day ahead of them.

And the man who had followed Kevin and Maureen called his superior and was told to maintain his watch.

This Man waited winter after winter as this sacred place above the cove began to change. First some cabins were built among the pines. And then a small log Chapel was built, right before the birch grove. It was the winter that the Chapel appeared that the first spirits joined This Man, and together they continued the song cycle.

In the morning they decided to retrieve Maureen's hired car from Toome; it was possible, Kevin contended and she acknowledged, that emerging circumstance might cause Maureen to bolt to the Dublin airport. Kevin was confident this townhouse was a well-protected secret; with so many coming and going since the previous evening, he preached caution now. Maureen left from the back door, scurried down the alley, and hid herself on the floor of the back seat of Kevin's car. Kevin arrived and drove out of town, giving her the all clear when it appeared no one was following. Maureen kept an eye on the road behind, and an eye on the road ahead.

She thought about calling Brian, but found she couldn't.

Kevin's contact waited five minutes and left from the front door, to drive to Banbridge where they would meet.

The man who had been watching the house saw Kevin leave, then a second man, and he waited for Maureen to show herself. The man grew suspicious, and ran to the alley behind the townhouse, but it was empty. And when he checked he found the townhouse appeared to be empty as well.

Before Brian headed to his booth in the ballroom for another day of playing Big Irish, the wilderness fishing camp owner, he stopped at the hotel front desk.

"Can you check for me again? I am expecting an overseas call."

"A call from Ireland as I recall."

"Yes, that's right."

"Let me check with the switchboard."

"It's a very important call, from Maureen Burke, my wife."

The hotel clerk left, was gone but a moment. "There's no record of any calls coming in from Ireland, and I've told all the operators to let me know as soon as one does."

"They need to let *me* know as soon as one does."

"Yes, sir."

Simon knew it was his job to awaken through the night to rebuild the fire and Trapper woke him when the fire burned low. Awake just before dawn, he wasn't surprised to see the snow falling through the smoke hole in the center of the wigwam's ceiling, for he had sensed the heavy quiet of a full snow fall coming on each time he woke to build the fire back. In the early gray light he pulled back the deer hide flap at the door and found the large flaked snow falling and filling the air so he couldn't see beyond the closest trees. Joe Loon sat up to look out over his grandson's shoulder, and he smiled. He told Simon to make sure they had wood for the morning for he was content to stay awhile, and he reached for his blanket to reposition himself so he could gaze out at the snow.

Trapper continued his prayer to the spirit of Beaver.

She was traveling five minutes behind Kevin; his contact told them of a quiet café down the street from the police station; each would reconnoiter the town separately and then meet at the café to find the best plan.

Maureen had packed her favorite pistol for this trip, a .38 caliber Smith & Wesson. The Model 40 was snub-nosed, light and compact, and she had not only practiced shooting cans and bottles at the garbage dump behind the Great Lodge until she was a deadeye expert shot, she practiced hiding it on her person. Now she took it out, from the loop she had sewn inside her coat sleeve, and placed it by her side. She picked it up every couple of minutes, to have a constant feel for it.

As she drove, she said a prayer. She prayed for justice and peace for Donovan O'Toole. She prayed for wisdom and for opportunity.

She prayed for forgiveness.

And she prayed that God bless the innocents.

❄ ❄ ❄

The heavy snowfall stopped by mid-morning. Joe Loon and Simon left their shelter and followed the last leg of their trap line up a slow and easy incline of the final ridge that separated them from the River and its new lake. Even with snowshoes it was a hard trudge through nearly a foot of fresh powder on top of a deep snow base; the binding on one of Simon's snowshoes was coming loose and he stopped to make a temporary repair.

They had the last of their traps tied to their packs.

Trapper walked just ahead of them.

They had one trap left that was sized for marten and found a number of promising spots as they worked their way up the ridge. Joe Loon told Simon to pick the spot he thought best, and then nodded his agreement as Simon laid the trap and placed the bait just right, and Joe Loon nodded again.

They still had three beaver traps between them, and as they approached the top of the ridge Joe Loon began calling to the spirits of this place, asking for their assistance discovering the secrets of where the big beaver had gone. Trapper joined him.

❄ ❄ ❄

Just before Maureen crossed the River she saw a road sign

pointing north, to Belfast, and she remembered that her father used to call Stormont "the kennels" because the Northern Irish government seated in Stormont were "Brit sheepdogs" trained to herd their sheep.

And after she crossed the River she felt certain, for the first time. If they could locate the man and if she was sure it was him, and if the opportunity was a clean one, she would shoot him.

No, she would kill him.

And on the heels of that certainty came the notion that, once successful, she *would* talk with Kevin about planning and leading another major raid, to turn the tide, all in the name of Donovan O'Toole.

She would urge they target Stormont.

Maureen entered Banbridge from the north and soon found her first objective, the police station. She drove by slowly, studying the two RUC officers standing outside. Theirs weren't familiar faces, but they were laughing, and it came to her suddenly that the men who gathered around her da when he was kneeling before his family, his face badly beaten, his hands tied behind his back, that those men had been laughing, right before they shot him.

No. Right before they killed him.

She drove on, slowing cruising all the side streets nearest the police station, alert for an officer's uniform. After she passed the police station a second time she finished her exploration of the town's streets and alleys, noting the dead ends, considering the hidden corners, making a mind map of the streets' patterns, as she'd been taught; she ended up at the café.

Joe Loon and Simon caught glimpses of the far shore of the lake before they rounded a forested knoll and looked down over the trees at the dam and a full view of the lake behind it. The strongest winds had been blocked on their side of the ridge. This side the winds whipped and howled, stirring up waves of the morning's snow from between the trees; some mighty gusts roared down the old River valley now filled with frozen lake, and the strong winds set the snow swirling again.

Trapper was on a different mission now, and he stayed at the top of the ridge when Joe Loon and Simon worked their way through the trees, the wind kicking up snow all about them.

"Grandfather, will these winds hide the signs and secrets you search for?"

"The winds may hide the signs. It could be a gust will carry the secrets to my ears."

Joe Loon pulled his scarf up over his nose and his hood down low as they reached the lake shore; the winds had rushed across the snow on the lake's ice since morning, creating low shifting drifts here, sweeping the ice clean there.

Joe Loon stepped out on the lake, just a step or two, to walk the ice along the shore, up stream, the dam behind him. Simon followed, but he stayed on shore, weaving between the spruce trees along the shoreline, only stepping on the ice when his route was fully blocked by dense growth and his snowshoe binding came loose again.

When they came to a grove of aspen they brushed away the snow from the base of the trees but didn't find any tooth marks. They continued some distance until Joe Loon stopped, pulled back his hood and lowered his scarf, and listened. He shook his head, covered up again, and they walked on.

The spruce along the ridge slope gave way to a sweep of maple trees and again they stopped to check for tooth marks. They found none, and Joe Loon asked, "Where have you gone?" When there was no answer Joe Loon decided it was time to turn around and head back to the wigwam.

This wasn't the first time Simon imagined what Maureen might do.

"She changes her view. She gets closer, or she stands back."

Simon stepped out onto the ice and kept heading out away from shore, sliding and stepping in his snowshoes, worried the binding was getting looser, and when he was ten yards out he turned.

"Before she would return, she would stand out here and look back at the shore."

Joe Loon followed and he pulled back his hood and lowered his scarf; the cold winds tossed his hair and froze the moisture around his eyes as he studied the forest and the ridge behind and above;

the wind burned the tips of his ears as he listened for whispers of something he could not hear.

After a minute he turned and Simon followed him further out on the lake, stopping thirty yards out, then walking another fifty yards, the wind bitter and sharp. After many minutes standing and watching and listening, Joe Loon was still searching.

When Joe Loon began to cover his head again Simon asked if they should walk to the very center of the long narrow lake, for a full look, all around, and at both shorelines. They walked together, first clattering on clear ice, then walking over small shifting sweeping drifts, for another ten or twenty yards, and when they got to the center of the lake they turned back to study the shore behind them and the trees swaying in the wind on the ridge, and the blue forever over the snow white and fir green world.

Simon's loose snowshoe slipped even more. As he turned to study the far shore he stomped his foot then pushed down, then stomped again and twisted his foot to jam his boot into the binding as far as he could; after this last stomp and twist a great dish of ice beneath them suddenly cracked and sagged and cracked some more, and just as the two began to move it broke away and they fell through the ice.

But they didn't fall into the freezing lake they had expected, and understood would mean a fearful death, strapped to so much dead weight in the icy cold water; instead they fell, and fell freely; they fell through space, through the air, waving and kicking next to each other, the broken ice from above falling around them, the snow from above showering them. They fell and landed with a hard thud on a rock solid surface that knocked all the wind and awareness out of Simon and crumbled the left ankle and jammed the right knee of Joe Loon before he then hit his head.

They lay still, side by side, nearly touching, but not moving.

Snow fell down on them, the sun shone down on them, from the hole in the ice above them.

Kevin and his man were waiting for Maureen when she arrived at the café. Kevin told him to share his information.

"I saw him enter the police station an hour ago."

"He's still there?"

"I got here five minutes before you. Saw you drive by twice, yeah. He was still there when I came to meet you."

"I'm goin' to find him."

"Wait a minute. Shouldn't we make a—"

"I appreciate that you found him here. But after what you told me last night I realized we don't know anything about his habits that would help me make a plan. So I'll find him an' watch for the opportunity."

As she stood Kevin placed his hand on her arm to keep her there.

"I don't like this."

"I have to do this now, Kevin. Right now."

"And when you're successful. Then what?"

She settled back in her chair.

Kevin had been writing on a paper when Maureen arrived. He slipped it to her. "A safe house, just across the border. Here's the directions. You head there and I will meet you."

She remembered this house, one they'd used when they were planning the second series of London bombing raids. She nodded her approval, handed the paper back to Kevin with a last half smile, and headed out the door and down the street towards the police station. The pistol was tucked in the loop in her sleeve.

Joe Loon and Simon lay still, next to each other, on their backs. They were so deeply shocked by the fall that nothing worked as it should and so they each lay there, just barely moving now.

Neither understood what had happened, or what was happening, or even what they were looking at when they finally opened their eyes, or where they were, for they were doubly stunned, by the impact of the fall, and by the sense, an emerging understanding, that the swirling colored lights around were the Path of Souls and so they might be dead.

Simon found the question forming on his lips but that was when the deep spasm hit him hard, for his lungs were demanding their first breath since the last he gasped just as the ice gave way, and it was a battle, it was coming hard, it hurt. His lungs wouldn't fill, couldn't fill, and he fought for that first breathe, so focused on this simple task, the pain in his lungs so great, that he had no capacity to clear his mind's confusion from the swirling dimensions of the world he'd fallen into.

Joe Loon lay still on his back, surprised he wasn't fighting for his life in the middle of a lake of freezing water, wondering if he had already lost the fight and this was his first gift from the next world, to forget his death pain as he takes his first steps along the Path of Souls, as he had never seen a world like this one, one that swirled around him, always changing its colors, dancing and leaping colors. Then the sharp pain in his leg seemed the pain of the world he lived in, and he wondered if it was some evidence they might still be alive.

Joe Loon was able to slip off one snowshoe, and hoped it would relieve some of the pain in his ankle, but it didn't. He pulled himself up on his side, towards Simon, but the pains running up and down his leg from his knee, and the way his vision wriggled and rolled when he lifted and turned his head as he looked past his immediate situation caused a deep sickness in him, and he quickly turned away from Simon as he gagged up what his stomach could no longer hold.

When he turned back again he realized that now they were on the hard thick ice that had covered the River and its lakes for well over a month, ice so thick it supported an ice tractor hauling sleds of logs. They were lying on the ice they thought they had walked out on.

Simon pulled his legs up and was finally gaining on the breath he'd been struggling to catch. As he did, he saw the blue sky above, framed by a hole in the great ceiling of ice, nearly twenty feet above them; the hole sent a bright shaft of white light that shined on them both. A few snowflakes drifted down.

They turned to each other. Joe Loon was moving his legs and rotating his feet to determine his injuries and found they were badly damaged.

Simon tried to sit up but it was still too soon, so he lay back down again.

"Grandfather."

They listened while the word rolled out as a hollow sound, not echoing, but lingering.

"Yes, my son."

"Are we dead?"

"I think we are alive, but I am not sure."

"What is this place?"

"I do not know."

Simon sat up next to him and understood for the first time that their island of white light was surrounded, all around, by a world of colored lights, of dancing swirls of colorful lights that were constantly twisting and folding and opening, shifting from blue to green, red crossing over yellow to blossom orange, so wondrous a dream world it scared and delighted him.

Joe Loon shook his head. "This is a place between worlds."

"Ah gee, I have never seen any place like this. So many colors of light. Is this the home of Waawaate?"

The sun's light shone through the ceiling of ice, a ceiling with cracks and fissures and constantly shifting snow, and each crack and dancing variance affected the light refracting through the ice ceiling, then that refracted light reflected up off the ice floor, and was again remade, prism of light woven with prism of light, creating shimmering and swirling dances of light in columns and bolts and waves and currents. A silver gray had a brilliant blue streak running one way, then a green blue cut running the other, then white light glowed a moment with a rose wave rolling through it that became bright red; and when a wisp of wind in the world above caused new fallen snow to twirl and drifts to reform, the lights danced their harmony in blue.

This dance of lights was all around the white shaft that spot lit the pair.

"The ice has trapped Waawaate."

"The Path of Souls passes through Waawaate."

They watched the lights dance and flow. The red became rose again then wrapped itself around a shaft of blue silver before it vanished.

"Grandfather. It is beautiful."

The sounds of their voices seemed to pause and hover, then join the dance of light all around.

There were other sounds. From just above, the crackling and tinkling, the crystalline snapping from the ice ceiling that sparkled overhead. And from far away, from some unknown distance, an echoed low rumble surrounded them.

"Is that low sound the voice of the dam Grandfather?"

"If that is the sound of the dam then I believe we are alive."

It was the purity of their ice floor that was the piece of the puzzle that told Simon what must have happened. He remembered their trip to the dam during the summer, and the loud horn announcing the release of water.

"When the River began to freeze the water trapped behind the dam wall was there." He pointed to their ice ceiling. "The ice began to form and became hard. But one day the dam let more water out. The water behind the dam had dropped down to this level when the full winter ice formed."

And it had formed perfectly protected from any distortion of the wind, no dimple or ruffles marked it, as absolutely smooth and slick a piece of ice that was ever created.

As Joe Loon studied the sleek surface he tried to look past the dancing lights; the thought came suddenly. He collected his legs under him to stand but the pain was so great he sat right back down again.

"My son, you must save us from this place. You must lead us out of this place between worlds. You must stand now and we must go."

Simon tried to get to his feet but his balance was lost, from the effects of the blow and the distortion of living in the heart of the shimmering lights of Waawaate, and because the ice was so slippery smooth. He stayed on his knees until Joe Loon urged him again.

"My legs are broken. I cannot stand on them. You must save us."

Joe Loon sat on the ice, the pain in his legs growing, and he collected his pack and the rifle and the last traps and his snowshoes all in a great pile in his lap. He had pulled a length of rope from under his coat and began to tie a loop in one end.

"We must find the way back to our world. We are not made for worlds between."

As he finished with the rope, he looked and listened.

"I have lost the four directions…listen for the voice of the dam."

After a moment listening, Simon pointed.

"It seems to be strongest in that direction Grandfather."

"Yes, so then the shore is in this direction."

Joe Loon put the loop of rope over his head, then under his armpits.

"I will be our sled; you will pull me."

Simon grabbed the rope with both hands behind him, leaned forward, and began to pull in the direction Joe Loon had pointed, slipping on ice so very slick it was tricky catching enough traction for forward momentum, but any traction he did achieve was productive, for Joe Loon slid easily, sitting backwards behind Simon with his lap piled high. They slowly made their way, out of the spotlight into the world of swirling shafts and columns and waves of colored lights dancing and shimmering, glowing and glimmering. The dam's deep rumbled purr and the icy bells above accompanied them as Joe Loon trailed his long length of scarf behind them to help them stay true to their course.

Watching the lights from the spotlight was fascinating. Now walking through them, bathed in them—the swirls and twirls enveloping one then the other, Simon bathed in blue and then bright red, Joe Loon yellow and then orange—this was fully befuddling, and Joe Loon was constantly calling course corrections as the scarf began to arc one way then the other.

Dutch, Mary Fobister, Grace O'Malley, and Little Stevie were finishing a late lunch when Brian stopped at their table. He gave his daughter a kiss then nodded for Dutch to step away with him for a moment.

"We're into the third day now without hearing from her."

"I don't know what to say Bri."

"God damn her. She promised to call every day; she knows there's no way for me to call her... I need to get back to the booth."

"As soon as we're through here I'll get them settled back in the room and come give you a hand."

It looked like him.

He was more than a block away, but from the distance it looked like it could be him. Maureen's heart was racing. An RUC officer was walking down the sidewalk, in her direction, and as soon as she saw him she thought it could be him. From this distance and with the brim of his hat covering so much of his face, she wasn't yet sure.

He hadn't been wearing a hat that day.

But it did look like him and with each step she was more confident.

She took a deep breath, for her heart was beating faster, and faster. She was accustomed to her state of deliberate calm as she prepared to act; now her adrenaline was winning and she was anxious for it.

She wanted to walk faster, she wanted to run, but her will won out and she maintained her steady stride as she wove her way through the pedestrians. She couldn't take her eyes off him, and she bumped into a woman, who frowned at the lady who wasn't watching where she was going and at the last moment a man stepped out of her way and smiled at her intense and otherworldly beauty.

But she didn't notice them, for the RUC officer was coming closer.

It was him; he stopped to talk with an old man and pushed his hat back and Maureen's knees nearly buckled. Faint, she leaned against a shop window, and took another deep breath.

She saw this man, pistol in his hand, standing over her da. She heard the crack of his pistol and saw her da's eyes empty and his body crumble to the ground.

Her anxiety was gone.

They were five yards from each other and Maureen collected herself when she felt the weight of the pistol against her arm; she was in control again, and she slipped the pistol gracefully, and quickly, from the loop into her hand, still hidden in the folds of her coat. Just as she began to imagine this moment as an opportunity and pictured shooting him right there, in the name of Donovan O'Toole, for all to witness, he turned away from the old man and walked back in the direction he came from, and then he turned at the first corner and disappeared down a side street. Maureen had driven down that street twice and she smiled at her recollection of it and what she found at the end of it.

She walked to the corner; the side street was as it had been when she drove it—quiet. There was a shop on either side right at the corner, but no action on the street or sidewalk except her target walking away past the abandoned buildings that dominated both sides of the street.

She studied the sidewalk traffic towards the police station, to see if any other RUC were around. Finding none, she followed him, for she had her plan for this opportunity. If he continued on as he was, and if no one appeared, she would pick up her pace—she did—and when he got to the end of the street she would catch up to him, and call out to him, and ask him a question about a location just around the next corner to the alley she remembered was fully deserted and offered her a hidden escape route. There, she would raise her pistol and shoot him in the head.

So she followed him, ready with the story that would explain where she was heading if he turned and engaged her, and constantly looking back over her shoulder.

Half way down the street her target stopped to check a locked door and she ducked in an entryway. When she peaked around the corner he was continuing on and she hadn't caught up with him by the time he turned the corner, so she came after him, silent and swift, her pistol ready in her hand, hidden in her coat pocket.

She turned the corner; he was gone, the back alley appeared empty.

"You lost, miss?"

She felt him behind her before he spoke, so she controlled her surprise and turned naturally, with a smile.

"Yes sir, can you help me." She pulled her pistol from her pocket. "I was looking for a—" And now the pistol was free and she raised it quickly with a practiced touch.

But he had been suspicious; he hadn't had time to wonder why this woman would be following him but instinct told him she was. So he was ready and he grabbed her arm in his firm grip and the pistol was pointed to the sky.

"Drop the—"

He was brought short by Maureen's hard knee to his groin; his face grew dumb and she wrenched her pistol hand away to take aim at his head. He reached for the gun and just before she pulled the trigger she closed her eyes, and the shot fired out, and she felt him drop at her feet. When she opened her eyes again, there he was, lying on his back, with a bullet hole right through his left eye, and a pool of blood forming a halo around his head. He kicked out once, and she prepared to shoot again, but when he kicked again it was his last.

The alley led to an empty lot, then another street that would lead her to her car. Without looking back again, she headed that way.

On her way to the safe house she would look for a phone box to get a message to her Mum, that she was sorry to miss her birthday but she wouldn't be home soon.

And she would try to call Brian.

❊ ❊ ❊

Simon stopped. He had grown accustomed to the lights; he thought he had learned to overcome their distraction. But now his confusion was back, for the strongest sound from the dam seemed to be ahead of them now.

"Grandfather, do you hear?"

Joe Loon heard, and had already called to the spirits who reside in the worlds between for help, and help was coming in a dark column of light that came spinning their way. As it approached, a darker shadow in the deep blue gray took shape and just as the column passed them, Joe Loon saw it quickly take the shape of a human's face that vanished the instant it formed. It was Hunter and his blue grey column of light passed them and rolled on, marking a new course for them to follow.

Joe Loon pointed Simon in that direction.

"You will lead us that way."

Simon had removed his snowshoes and was learning how to press against the inside edges of his boots to most effectively catch some friction to push off and pull his grandfather across the ice, but still the progress was slow, and often a step slipped by with no gain.

After a few minutes Simon stopped again. He thought he saw

something move in the lights, ahead and off to the side. He stepped back to help his grandfather turn around to see.

"There is something coming towards us."

"Yes."

The shadow moved through the shifting lights, and as is it did a second and much larger shadow took shape behind it. Their course was not easy to ascertain with the lights all around always swirling and twirling and floating back and opening wide, and always changing colors. The two shadows moved slowly through veils of light that obscured, until the next step of the first shadow showed itself to be a wolf and Simon took a peek at his grandfather to gauge his reaction. The wolf trotted a path through the lights, a blue wolf one moment, then green, and then his natural silver seemed to glow with fire as a shimmer of rose washed over him.

The larger shadow followed behind, they slowly came closer, and while his grandfather was calm Simon noted he had his hand on the rifle.

The second large shadow emerged. It was a moose, bathed in green, laboring to keep up but following the wolf on a course that led them both closer and closer to Joe Loon and Simon.

The wolf trotted, his head red, his body blue, and then red head to tail, until without any apparent recognition he changed his path slightly as he passed by, his head slung low, his tongue hanging out. He barely glanced at the men, and never broke his dogtrot, and the big blue moose followed, ten yards back, on limping and wobbling legs. Joe Loon and Simon watched them pass by and head on their way, the moose following the wolf together, changing colors constantly, until they vanished in the lights.

"They were lost until they found each other."

Simon grabbed the rope and turned Joe Loon around and continued their slow progress through this world, trying to get home to their world.

On her way to the car Maureen joined the street disturbed by the early rumors that someone had been shot, perhaps a police officer. Kevin's man stepped in next to her as she passed by and asked if she needed anything. She nodded no and he drifted back.

She was confident she hadn't been seen, but she wasn't certain. She was tempted to join the crowd that was heading closer to the scene of the shooting to learn what she could, and that's when it was Kevin's turn to approach her, though he didn't acknowledged her. Once he knew she saw him he walked behind her, just off her shoulder.

"I'll follow you to your car to see if anyone else is."

They walked away from the action and soon the sidewalks were empty. Still, they were careful. As they drew near to her car Maureen spoke for the first time.

"He nearly bested me Kevin. He must of figured I was followin' him an' he had my arm an' we struggled… An' then… I closed my eyes, yeah. At the last moment, as I was pullin' the trigger… I didn't want to know his name… I didn't want to see him get shot… I just wanted him dead… I just wanted to avenge Da's death… "

They got to the car and Kevin kneeled down at the curbside rear tire, acting as if he were inspecting it.

"I have to go to Derry. Something's come up I need to attend to. I'll be back by tomorrow afternoon."

"Will you have a chance to look in on Mum? I don't know if she's gotten any of my messages an' she was worried when I left."

"Yes, I can do that."

"Tell her I'm fine an' wish her a happy birthday an' tell her I've got good news for her when I see her."

The sacred spot continued to change as winter followed winter. There were more cabins among the pines. Then a large log structure appeared; it was twice as tall as the other cabins and many times bigger. A new dock was built, one that extended out into the cove, and two buildings sat at the end of the dock. And still This Man repeated the song cycle as more and more spirits joined him.

And then the spirit of Mathew Loon, the River's true warrior, joined them in their call.

It was near dusk when Maureen left Banbridge. She was alert to any car following her and when one did pull out behind her she decided to change her route and headed north. The other car drove off to the east but she continued north, not south to the safe house, and unsure why. She drove on and when she got to the River, near Dromore, she turned west, and followed it. In the last light she pulled off to the side of the road and walked down to the River and stood at the shore.

She watched the River flow, its surface black and slick.

She had accepted that smuggling bomb making materials into London years earlier could result in people being killed, and when two men died from the first mission, and one more from her second, she accepted she had a role in their deaths. And she knew when they executed the Ebrington Barracks raid that she might be called upon to shoot someone; she had convinced herself and Kevin then that she was ready to shoot a man straight on if it came to that.

But this was the first time she had. This was the first time she pointed a gun and pulled the trigger and shot a man and watched him die.

"He weren't no feckin' innocent," she said to the River, and spat out the bad taste in her mouth.

She decided to continue, to meet Kevin at the safe house and craft a plan for an IRA victory that hit the Brits in their heart, not just in Belfast but Stormont itself. If Kevin could help her identify and plan an operation that could be executed now, in the next couple of days, she was ready. She got back in her car, returned to the main road, and suddenly the full weight of not calling Brian hit her so she detoured to Dromore to find a phone box.

Night was falling as Maureen drove into Dromore, a small market town. She saw the Catholic church, St. Colmans, and parked to go inside. The church was empty; she walked to the front of the church and kneeled in front of the altar, and prayed. When she left she found a phone box, and called the hotel in Chicago where the fishing shows were being held. When the hotel operator answered, Maureen asked her to ring Brian Burke's room.

"He's been expecting your call."

"Pardon me."

"My manager let me know that when you called, I was to make sure I got you connected with him."

"Then please ring me through."

There was no answer, and Maureen waited for the hotel operator to come back on the line.

"Tell him his wife called, that she sends her love, that all is fine, an' I will call him in the mornin'."

"He'll be disappointed he missed you, but I'll make sure he gets this message as soon as he returns. Is there a number he can call you?"

"No, I'm afraid not."

"Would you like me to ring the front desk and see if they can find him? Perhaps they're having an early supper in our restaurant."

"No, I'm at a phone box, a pay phone, an' I really do need to be movin' on."

As Maureen drew close to the border between the County Armagh and County Louth—leaving British Northern Ireland and entering the Free Republic—she turned on the headlight's high beams, anticipating something very like what she found as she rounded a curve: barriers blocking the road on the British side of the border, though there were many more men than she imagined—a half a dozen uniformed RUC and a couple in civilian dress.

They stood alert as her car approached. She slowed and drove closer. She checked her pistol; it was holstered in the coat sleeve loop.

An RUC officer separated himself from the rest to walk up the road toward her, squinting in her bright headlights, and he waved her to stop. She slowed, then stopped. Many of the men turned their backs to her lights or held their arms in front of their faces, the high beams were intense, and they yelled at her to turn off her lights. She acted as if she didn't hear them as she rolled down her window.

The officer approached, his hand up to block the light.

"Turn off your lights Miss."

She turned off her car, but left the lights on, and opened the door to get out when he shouted angrily.

"Turn off your lights now!"

"You've no reason to raise your voice with me. An' you better have *good* reason for stoppin' a woman at night."

She turned off her lights and the men relaxed. Just before she got out of the car she decided to leave the pistol under the car seat, then she stepped out.

"Just what are you doing all alone on the road at night?"

"Are you tryin' to intimidate me? My attorney will be very interested in how, do I count seven, how seven men treat one woman all alone on the road so late at night."

"Your attorney is it now."

"Confirm my count. Five RUC's, yes that's right, an' them two in suits. What should I call them, your friends in civilian garb?"

Maureen had removed her Canadian driver's license from her purse before she got out of the car, and she thrust it in the man's face, waited for him to see what it was, then continued.

"Folks in Canada, they ask me if I left this country because of the Brits. I tell them it's their Proddie sheepdogs that spoiled the land an' sickened me." She took a couple of steps towards the other men. "Let me ask these fine gentlemen. Is there one Roman Catholic among your ranks?"

One of the men called out, "Shut 'er up."

She turned back to the officer.

"An' now it's your men threatenin' me for askin' an innocent question? Why don't you ask one a them to start makin' a list of their names for me."

The officer turned to his men.

"Let her through. Get in your car and get out of here."

She smiled and walked back to the car. "You gotta hand that to the Brits, they know how to train sheepdogs."

"Now."

She got in her car, started the engine, and her headlights came on in high beam. She drove through the opening in the barricade, the men calling her out as she passed.

"I think I can see shore through the lights ahead."

As the shore took shape Simon did not like what he saw. He turned Joe Loon around to see the solid rock wall, running straight up from the ice floor to the ice ceiling.

Joe Loon stared at the wall for a few moments, remembering

the rock faced bluff along and above the River's old shoreline, there forever, before the dam was built. He pictured the shore on both sides of the rock wall, then told Simon which direction they should follow the shore.

After they traveled a short distance Simon told Joe Loon, "There is something ahead…it's laying on the ice."

The spectrum of ice light had slowly grown darker—the blues and greens darker until absorbed in the gray, the reds and yellows almost gone—so they had to be close before they were sure it was a deer, lying on its side, dead.

They passed by the full carcass, not killed apparently, simply dead. They continued following the face of the rock wall, and soon passed another dead deer.

The farmhouse where Maureen and Kevin would stay while they planned their next moves was still an hour away, and the last distance was down a side road. She pulled off the side road into the yard and parked the car around behind the house, out of view of the road, retrieved the key from the small flowerpot nearest the door, and went inside. Her exhaustion was profound; she'd slept no more than a couple of hours here and there since she left Canada, nearly four days ago. She pulled out her notebook and began to jot down some questions and ideas for a raid on Stormont, but when she realized she'd dozed off while sitting up, she knew it was time to find a bed.

The hotel operator was right: Brian and Dutch, along with Mary Fobister and the children, had been eating supper at the hotel diner when the call from Maureen came in. Brian checked with the front desk on their way up to their rooms and found the message. His anxiety was replaced by his anger. He was angry at the hotel for not coming to get him, and he was angry at himself for not thinking to tell them he was close by should she call; but mostly he was angry at Maureen, for failing to do as she promised, for failing to act as his wife and Grace's mother should. He was angry that this trip of hers scared him so.

With Mary watching over the sleeping children—Grace and Little Stevie shared a bed with each other and a room with Mary—Brian and Dutch were in the hotel bar, the bar and tables filled with camp owners and outfitters. The room was loud with laughter and grand proclamations. Brian and Dutch were sipping whiskey—Brian the Irish, Dutch a Canadian blend. Brian still held the note about Maureen's call in his hand.

"What about Gracie. Forget about me, what about Gracie?"

"I don't know what to say that'll soothe you Brian. She's as independent a woman as I've ever met."

"Which was fine when it was her an' me an' no one else."

He finished the last in his glass and slammed it hard against the wood tabletop.

"God damn her."

"That's the second time you've done that Brian, damned her. He just might be listening and think you mean it one of these times."

"Of course I don't mean it." He waved to the bartender, got his attention, and signaled for two more. "Just God damn what she's doin' to me, that's all."

❄ ❄ ❄

The lights in the ice world had continued to change, and now all the color was gone; the darker aspects dominated as the sun set in the world above.

The rock wall gave way to a slope that had been spruce forest before a lumber company logged the trees that would be flooded by the dam. Simon and Joe Loon studied the incline in the last of the light; the stumps offered themselves as something like steps except every bit of every surface, the stumps and the forest floor between them, and the logging remnants scattered all around, all of it was covered in a sheet of ice.

Joe Loon unloaded his lap, put on his pack, slung the rifle over his shoulder, and clipped the traps to a strap. He leaned to grab a stump. "I will pull myself up."

As they searched for a course up the steep slope among the stumps the growing darkness obscured more and more detail.

Simon found the ice was treacherously slick, the footing precarious, and he slipped feeling for first footholds. He started again, and they were both making slow progress when Simon slipped again and fell down onto Joe Loon, knocking them both down onto the ice floor; Simon landing on top of his grandfather. When Joe Loon's knee hit the ice he cried out in full pain for the first time.

"I am sorry Grandfather."

"Yes. Yes, you should be sorry."

It was nearly total darkness; dusk was giving way to night. Joe Loon sat up and leaned out to feel for the shore.

"We must not spend the night in between. When we climb out we are alive. If we stay here, we are dead."

Again they started to climb, Joe Loon reaching out blindly for any handhold, his hands searching, searching, grabbing and pulling, pushing to reach again, resting each step along the way, his knee burning and his ankle throbbing. Simon was on all fours, secured what felt to be a firm base, then lay on his belly to reach out for the next advance.

They made their way slowly, unsteadily, each foot of progress hard won, stopping to rest often, for they were exhausted before they began. When Simon's arm slipped from under him and his head hit an ice-sheeted rock, he turned into a ball at the pain and slid down until he slammed into a tree stump that caught him; again, the wind was knocked from him. This time it felt everything was knocked from him.

He heard Joe Loon's voice above him.

"We must keep climbing."

But Simon couldn't keep climbing. His head was pounding. His head was spinning. His whole body ached. His whole body was exhausted. He wanted to rest right there. He needed to rest right there.

"We must keep climbing." Joe Loon's voice was insistent, but Simon didn't hear it as he faded into a barely conscious state.

Below in the dark, there was a movement. Was a shadow taking shape and moving? Yes, and it came closer, slowly, but closer and closer.

It was Grandmother. She wore fur-lined skins, with a Hudson Bay blanket over her head and shoulders. As she approached

Simon, she sang a song to the spirits of this place, and as she sang she covered him in her blanket. Soon Simon stirred, and he realized where he was and that he had to try again, though it seemed so peaceful he wanted to stay; he took a deep breath to enjoy the peace.

Grandmother lifted her blanket, covered herself again and, still singing, continued on up the slope. Simon took a deep breath that called to his last reserves but shot deep pains to his back and his side, and it hurt even more when he reached in the dark for a handhold. Once he found one he made sure he was secure, and then he started climbing, and kept climbing, his back blazing in pain with each reach.

Simon and his grandfather both kept climbing, they had to keep climbing, groping in the dark, learning what could be learned about the balance needed on ice-covered stumps and rocks, but making painfully slow progress for they each feared their next slip could be their last.

Just before Joe Loon reached the ice ceiling Simon caught up with him, and they finally broke through the ice together and climbed out, exhausted, to lay next to each other—in the snow, on the shore, breathing hard, confident for the first time that they were alive. Joe Loon attended to the pain in his legs by chanting his thanks to the spirits who helped save them. Simon's head was throbbing, sharp pains attacked his back, and he removed his mittens to discover he had a frozen gash of blood at his hairline. Just then a break in the clouds opened and the moon shone brightly, so they both sat up to look out over the ice.

"We will build a shelter here for I cannot travel. In the morning you will go for help. It is nearly two days to Grassy in this snow."

"I will go to the dam first to see if anyone there can help us."

"Are there men at the dam? We did not see any men."

"There must be men in one of those buildings. I will go there first to search for help."

Just above them was a large boulder jutting out from the ground at the edge of the thick low boughs of a spruce. Simon pulled his grandfather up to it, and they dug away at the snow under the bough and formed the snow into walls, using the boulder as one wall of the shelter. Simon cut away branches with the hatchet and

Joe Loon arranged them with their blankets as beds on the snow floor of their shelter and to prop against the wind.

Simon collected wood and started a fire, while Joe Loon offered small portions of the smoked fish from their provisions. After they ate, Simon cut more boughs, and while Joe Loon used them to improve their beds and shelter Simon cut more firewood.

Again, Simon prepared to care for the fire throughout the night.

All the clouds had blown away, and the sky was filled with bright stars and a nearly full moon, and the night was the dead of winter cold.

While Joe Loon slept Simon was fighting to stay awake to tend the fire. Grandmother sat at the fire, with Young Sister. They were covered in her blanket and furs; Simon stirred the flames and watched the twisting flurry of sparks spiraling up into the stars.

Finally, exhausted, Simon fell asleep. Grandmother looked after the fire and wakened him when it needed more wood.

Chapter 8
MISSIONS PLANNED AND EXECUTED

IT WAS APPROACHING NOON before Maureen woke. She found little in the pantry but a box of stale biscuits. She slipped a few in the pocket of her coat, washed out a bottle to fill with water, left a note for Kevin, then stuffed the pad of paper and pencil in her pocket with the biscuits. She thought to go back to the bedroom for a blanket then slowly walked up the easy slope of the pasture behind the farmhouse. When she crested the rise and looked out over the next fields, she could see at a distance the grove of trees that was her destination.

At the edge of the grove, just across the property line of the Ballymascanlon Hotel, sat a Neolithic tomb, the massive Proleek Dolmen.

The dam was over a mile from their shelter in roughly the same direction Simon would travel to return to Grassy Narrows. They decided if Simon didn't find anyone at the dam he would continue on to the Reserve; if he wasn't back by evening with help from the dam workers, Joe Loon would plan to be alone for two or three days.

As the sun rose Simon chopped enough wood for Joe Loon's fire for four days. They divided their remaining matches and blankets and food, then Joe Loon gave Simon his scarf and the rifle.

"You keep the rifle Grandfather."

"No, you must take it."

"If I must travel on to the Reserve I travel as light as I can."

"You will take my scarf for your eyes."

Simon's eyes had always watered more than others in the cold wind, so he wrapped his grandfather's scarf around his head, covering much of his face, but he didn't take the rifle.

They prayed together, touched each other, and Simon headed off down the shoreline towards the dam. Grandmother stayed with Joe Loon, to watch over him.

There was a light snow falling, the wind was calm. Simon would follow the shoreline to the dam—they decided he would stay off the ice—and when he got to the dam he hoped to find someone to help them.

He had traveled about half way, walking over and through a deep snow bank, pain from his back accompanying each step, when the binding broke on the same snowshoe that had caused the trouble on the ice; he lifted his foot, the snowshoe dangling by the toe strap only. He tried to wedge his boot deeper in the toe strap but that helped for only twenty or thirty yards before it became so loose that the snowshoe slipped off all together. Simon retrieved it, then staggered and hopped through the knee-high snow to step out on the ice. He took the other snowshoe off, tied them to his pack, and walked on the ice right at the shore, in a slow gliding motion that relieved much of the pain in his back, listening anxiously for cracking ice.

Maureen walked around the Dolmen, studying it from all angles. The megalithic portal tomb looked like a giant three-stemmed toadstool, a tripod of vertical stones holding up its capstone, altogether twice the height of a man. She could see a good portion of the surface of the Dolmen's cap, and she wondered how it had become dotted with the warts of so many stones sitting atop the capstone. She decided they looked like they belonged there as part of a fairy tale.

She found a place to spread her blanket and removed the items from her coat, laying the water bottle, the biscuits, her note pad, some loose sheets, and one envelope with both packets Kevin had sent on the blanket in front of her. She read them all again, in the light of the previous day's events, making notes as she did. She pulled papers out of the notepad to rearrange them. She finished her reading, set it aside, and took another walk around the Dolmen.

When she sat down again she started writing a letter to her mum, telling her what she had done. Then she made a list of what she needed to know from Kevin about his organization and she reviewed her first thoughts about a mission against Stormont. She got up again for another trip around the site then sat down to note what had come to her.

On her third trip around the tomb a plan began to take shape; she soon found she had too many questions for Kevin before she was confident enough to finish it. But she considered the work a promising start; Stormont was in her sights.

✳ ✳ ✳

The same two men who met there two days earlier were back at the Giant's Causeway, and their argument about whether Maureen had been positively identified was growing more heated.

"So tell me again."

"Feck you, it don't get no different in the retelling of it."

"Tell me again."

"One of my lads tailed her out of Derry, with a second car behind him. The second lad tailed her to a meeting with Kevin at Toome Bridge and caught up with her again in Antrim in time to see Kevin enter a townhouse, then she entered, then over the next thirty minutes or so, four more of Kevin's brigade entered one at a time. They were all together there for a little over an hour. After the first men left, one more arrived."

"Your boys must be telling you what you want to hear."

"What makes you so goddamn sure? I think you're just trying to keep from paying my boys what's due, taking the info but holding the pounds."

"I'll tell you what makes me so goddamn sure. I already knew of Kevin's meeting in the townhouse in Antrim. One of Kevin's brigade who was in that meeting is one of my lads, you see. I have my own infiltrators I'm taking care of, you see. And he says no, she wasn't at that meeting."

"And my lad says she was, that he saw her go in, that she spent the night there, and in the morning she must have snuck out the back alley way, and if I go back and tell him he don't get paid for his day's work, his night's work, he's gonna want to know who it is that's calling him a liar."

"If he's so sure he can actually lay eyes on her, tell him he can fiddle around with a few pounds for information, or he can come see Jerry and me about a big reward."

"What big reward?"

"The kind that comes when we give the fellows in Stormont and London absolute proof she was here, but that this trip will be the last one she'll ever make."

"If it's an action worth doing your meaning could be clearer."

"If you're right, if she's here, well that means the only London bomber gone unpunished has made a return trip home. Some would be very happy if they were to know for certain that all them feckin' Fenian murderers have been punished."

The wind grew stronger all morning and now it howled across the lake. Snow was falling at a hard angle, the treetops swayed in circles, and a sudden hard wind gust nearly swept Simon off his feet.

He rounded a point of land and the wind roared right in his face; his eyes watered so much he could barely make out the dam and the buildings on either side of it. The dam was still two hundred yards away.

Simon stepped up on shore, behind a tree, to get protection from the wind, to wipe his eyes, to rest his back. As he studied the dam, he reached inside his coat, then inside his shirt, and pulled out some venison jerky wrapped in a cloth. He took a small bite and chewed it deliberately while he studied the outbuildings. He took a second bite, put the meat away, then took two or three mouths full of freshly fallen snow.

He would stay on shore the rest of the way, even if it meant plowing through drifts waist high, knowing that would make his back pain even worse, but the thought of falling through the ice so close to the dam terrified him. He pushed his way through the snow, studying the new angles and sight lines of the dam and its buildings as he approached, looking for any signs of habitation, finding none.

It began snowing even harder.

❋ ❋ ❋

When Maureen returned to the farmhouse, she found Kevin had arrived and was in the kitchen putting away the supplies he purchased. He had hardly stopped moving since Maureen saw him the day before in Banbridge and hadn't slept at all, driving to Derry and back, and he looked even more haggard than before. He paced from the box of supplies on the table to the cupboard, and back again, filled with nervous tension, retrieving one item from the box, putting it away, absently, and then another, one item at a time.

"I got bad news Lady Girl."

Maureen showed panic. "Mum's all right."

He stopped and took a breath to collect himself the best he could.

"Sorry, yes, sorry, no I looked in on her and she's fine."

"Jaysus, Kevin, you taught me better… Now sit down, will you, you're makin' me nervous. You're exhausted."

He sat.

"Then what is it?"

"We lost two, last night, we lost two of our best. Not from my unit, from the Armagh brigade. The mine they were planting on some railroad tracks exploded as they were placing it."

"Bad makin's or sabotage?"

Kevin stood. "Some says one, some says the other. I'm going to call one of mine who has been checking it out. If it's sabotage… well, we need to find out who the infiltrator is."

"When you return my presence will still be a kept secret?"

"That's right."

"My Mum have any message for me?"

Kevin was at the door, stopped, shook his head in embarrassment again, and came back to deliver the news.

"Yes, yes she did. I'm sorry, Maureen, I'm just so worn out right now. She said to tell you to take care, to do what's right, and to come home to her when you're finished with your mission."

"She said that?"

"That's right."

"She said when I finish my mission."

"That's right."

"So you didn't tell her what's done already?"

"That's yours to tell, not mine."

Simon pounded on the metal door of the first building he came to at the dam site, a cinder block box. There was no answer. He walked around the building, but the windows were small and placed too high for him to see in, and there was no other door. He could not imagine anyone would live in such a building, and his were the only tracks in the fresh snow, but he pounded on the door one more time.

Across the dam, on the other side of the River, was a second and much bigger building. Though the snow kept falling hard, Simon thought he could see a light on at the larger building. He hesitated before he stepped out onto the walkway that led across the top of the dam. He took one step and waited. Then he walked quickly. The wind kept roaring, blowing the snow into his face.

There was a hum from the dam that he felt in the vibrations that entered his body through his feet. Simon stopped in the middle of the walkway, for while it was bitterly cold, the weather's fury and the dam's power had filled and then thrilled his body, and he breathed deeply the freezing air, adding to the rush of it all. He looked out over the frozen lake and tried to find where Joe Loon's shelter was, but the falling snow blocked sight of the lakeshore well before. He slowly punched his fist in his grandfather's direction, shaking his fist a bit while he held his arm at full extension, and he repeated the move four times, shouting while sending the dam's tremendous energy across the lake against the winds to his grandfather in his shelter.

His back pain was spiking again, so he walked slowly to the end of the dam and approached the larger building. He followed a series of tracks in the snow that were nearly enveloped in the newly fallen snow; they led him to the door—there was a light on just above the door—and he knocked, waited, then pounded it hard.

There was no answer.

He waited, then pounded it one more time.

When no one came, Simon followed another set of old tracks

around the corner of the building to discover a Willy's Jeep, with a snow blade, parked behind the building at the end of a one-lane construction road that needed to be plowed before anyone would be able to travel it through the forest to the highway. The Jeep was covered in snow.

Simon returned to the door and pounded twice more, but there was still no answer, so he returned to the Jeep, found the door unlocked, and climbed in for a respite from the wind and snow.

He was very cold. And sitting lessened some of his back pain.

He untied the broken snowshoe from his pack and examined the busted binding. He looked around the Jeep for something he could use to fix it. He did not want to spend the next two days walking through snow that was knee high, even waist high in places, without snowshoes—he knew his pain was worse when he walked through the snow—but if he returned to Joe Loon to borrow his grandfather's snowshoes he'd lose a day.

He searched the Jeep thoroughly and when he couldn't find anything to fix the binding, in frustration and in pain, he pounded on the steering wheel, surprised when he inadvertently hit the horn and it sounded a short blast.

Now his hands hurt too, and his anger grew. To keep from pounding the steering wheel again he grabbed it and shook it, hard, again and again, and he cocked his head to look up and howl a long call of painful rage. Then he pressed the Jeep's horn to honk it loud and long to accompany his second call.

Then he stopped, he had to, his back was tightening, and slowly he regained control; he began to calm down as the energy in his anger dissipated and the worst of the pain receded.

He was collecting his things to leave the Jeep to try each door one more time before he headed back for Joe Loon's snowshoes, when around the corner appeared two white men in white overalls and light blue hard hats.

Each white man had a rifle and one was pointing it, if not at Simon, certainly towards him. Simon held his hands in clear view, while the other white man opened the Jeep door and Simon stepped out, holding his hands out, palms up.

"The son of a bitch was trying to steal the Willys."

"He was trying to hot wire it and got the wrong wires crossed and set off the horn instead."

"That's what it looks like to me."

"I do not know how to drive."

"He could be lying about that as easy as they lie about how they'll spend that dollar they're begging you for."

"You must have heard me knock on the door. I wanted you to know I am here. So you can put away your rifles. I will do no harm."

"We heard you and figured you'd just go away. And you figured no one was here so you could steal the Willys, eh?"

"I cannot steal it. I do not know how to drive it. I have come to ask for your help."

The men lowered their rifles.

"What kind of help?"

"My grandfather has a trap line along that ridge—"

"We own that ridge now. You redskins shouldn't even be up there."

"You own Waabizheshi? It has always been a place where my people… My grandfather hurt both his legs and cannot walk. He waits for me in a shelter we built on the shore."

"You're not supposed to be trapping up on the ridge and you sure as hell aren't building any shelters on the shore, not anymore. Ontario Hydro owns the land you're standing on and pretty much all the land you can see from where you stand, and you're breaking the law if you're on our land for any reason. It's called trespassing."

"I understand what you are saying."

"Is that right? Hear that, Oscar, he understands me. Well then go fetch your grandfather and make sure he understands and you both clear on out of here."

"And tell all the other redskins we're off limits from now on."

"I will tell everyone I meet what you have taught me. But now I will ask you to understand me. My grandfather cannot walk. His legs are badly hurt. We would like to leave your ridge, but we will need your help."

"It'll take more than a busted up old Indian to get me out in this snowstorm. How far away is he?"

Simon stepped back to have the view past the building he

needed and pointed across the lake. "On the shore line across the lake in that direction."

"I don't think the company would approve of us leaving our posts anyhow."

"You have a radio?"

"And a telephone. Who would you be calling?"

"Do you know Big Brian Burke?"

"Big Brian?"

"He owns The Great Lodge at Innish Cove."

"I know who Brian Burke is."

"My grandfather and Big Brian are father and son now. The men of my grandfather's village built the fishing camp and they work there as his best fishing guides. I will use the telephone to call Big Brian, and he will send help for my grandfather."

"Who's Brian Burke?"

"You know who he is. It was him and his wife who were tying us up in court there for a while, that cut the one build season in half."

"I will use your phone to call for his help. So we can leave your land."

"Come on in."

They entered and walked down a hall. Simon pulled down his hood and unwrapped the scarf from around his head. One of the men noticed the big gash across the corner of his forehead; it was scabbing over and bruised and swollen.

"What happened to your head?"

"In the dark last night I fell on a rock."

There was a telephone on a desk and a two-way radio on the table next to it.

"I could use your phone to call for help. Then I could use your radio to talk to my people at Grassy Narrows."

"Who has a radio at Grassy Narrows?"

"There is a Hudson's Bay Post at Grassy. They have a radio."

One man picked up the phone and rang for the operator.

"What's Big Brian's phone number?"

When Simon first began traveling and spending time with Brian and Maureen, they had him memorize a telephone number to use if he ever needed them in an emergency.

"The number I have is for Big Brian's lawyer. He is named Tom Hall."

The operator was on the line.

"Yes, just a second. What's the number?"

"Kenora 4552."

The operator connected the call as the man handed the phone to Simon. He listened to it ring and ring and ring. He had never called the number though he had visited Tom Hall's law offices a number of times with Maureen, or Brian, or both of them; as the phone continued to ring he realized it was Saturday and he had learned white men are not in their offices on Saturday. He was about to give up when a woman answered.

"McCormick, Hall, and Roberts."

"Hello. I am calling for Tom Hall?"

"He's not here."

"Big Brian Burke told me to call him when I have an emergency message for him."

"Who is this?"

"I am Simon Fobister. I am the grandson of Joe Loon. Big Brian said if I ever needed his help, I should call this number and ask for Tom Hall."

"This is Simon?"

"Yes, I am Simon."

"Sure, we've met when you've been in the office. You say it's an emergency?"

"Yes."

"Well, you see, Mr. Hall was in this morning for a partners meeting but they've all just left. You're lucky to catch me here, I was just ready to leave as well. Mr. Hall should arrive at his home in the next ten minutes or so. I will call his house and explain it is urgent that he call you as soon as he gets in."

Simon turned to the white men.

"She is going to have Tom Hall call me here in ten minutes."

"Let me tell her how he'll ring us up, eh."

A few minutes later Tom Hall called, learned what had happened, and promised to call Brian right away. Then Simon radioed the Hudson's Bay Post, asked the shopkeeper to name who was in the store, and they identified someone who could get the message to Albert Loon that Simon needed to speak with him.

While they waited for the return calls, one of the white men fetched the first aid kit to clean and bandage Simon's head wound. Then Simon asked them if they had leather cord or strong twine so he could repair his snowshoe.

Brian stood at the table set up to promote both The Great Lodge at Innish Cove and North Ontario Airlines. There were over a hundred tables for lodges and camps, outfitters and guides, organized row after row, and the aisles were filled with fathers and young sons, fathers and adult sons, old fishing buddies, new fishing buddies, hunt club members, very few wives, and even fewer daughters.

Brian was leafing through a photo album with a father and his boy; he used his Big Irish accent to tell them about the wilderness fishing experience that awaited them at The Great Lodge at Innish Cove.

He turned to the last pages of the album to show the photograph of Ernest Hemingway, holding his trophy northern pike, and the father turned to the boy.

"You're looking at the world's greatest outdoorsman, Guy. That's Ernest Hemingway, the writer. He loves to hunt, he loves to fish, and then he writes great stories about it."

"This photo is from this past summer, in August. He says he's comin' back again next season—" Brian was interrupted by a man in a hotel jacket.

"I'm sorry, Mr. Burke, but there's a phone call at the front desk. They say it's an emergency."

Brian left the father and son standing there as he turned quickly to step rapidly, weaving his way through the crowded aisles; he called back over his shoulder to the man in the hotel jacket.

"Who's callin'?"

The man in the hotel jacket was trying to keep up but was losing ground.

"Pardon me?"

"I said who called?"

"I don't know."

Brian walked faster as he roared and heads turned, and the crowd parted for him.

"You don't know! Who said it was an emergency?"

"Sorry, they didn't tell me, they just said to find you, fast."

Brian left the ballroom to cross the lobby to the front desk. There was a look of concern on the woman's face as she stood behind the counter; he got madder still as he snatched the phone from her hand when she offered it.

To her he said, "Go get your manager!" and to the phone he said "It's Brian."

He was greatly relieved when he heard it wasn't bad news about Maureen. He listened to all his attorney knew about Joe Loon and Simon's predicament, and when Tom Hall finished he remembered that the Ontario Department of Lands and Forests had Bell 47 helicopters, and that at least one was outfitted with pontoons. They could fly in and get them, if they would fly in and get them.

"I know a good man named Dillon, the Regional Fire Protection Supervisor within the Department. I'll track him down as quick as I can and see if I can make the case for a rescue with him."

"Thanks. Keep me appraised."

The two dam operators had listened in when Simon described to Tom Hall about the two layers of ice and how they were formed and how Joe Loon's injury occurred and about their escape from the world between. When Simon was off the phone one white man finished bandaging his head, the other one asked to hear more about what it was like to be in between the two layers of ice.

"Yaway, it was a beautiful dream place. But it was frightening. I thought we were dead. My grandfather wasn't sure. We thought this was the beginning of the journey on the Path of Souls traveling through Northern Lights."

"Really?"

"The lights are dancing and swirling all around you. Blue light and green. Red lights. This should be called Rainbow Lake... ah, gee, it was beautiful."

"Wow. We got to check this out, eh Pete. Let's go down in there, in between the ice, tomorrow, once the storm has passed."

Simon shook his head. "You do not want to do that."

"Why not?"

"It was beautiful. Ah gee, it was very beautiful. But you feel trapped in between. Then you feel the death there and you have to get out."

"Na, that's just how you felt because at first you thought you were dead."

"Yeah, if I knew I could get out, then I wouldn't feel trapped."

"I have not told you about the animals."

"What animals?"

"There are animals trapped in between that cannot get out."

"What did you see?"

"Many dead deer. There was a moose that was so afraid in this world in between he was following a wolf for comfort. Those who lived here before this dam was built, the forest animals, and us, we are all confused by what is happening to our home. Now there are animals dying because they are hurt when they fall through the ice and they are trapped in between."

"Ah, how many?"

"When did you drop the water from the highest level?"

"Jesus, it was about a month ago."

"We saw many dead. We saw others dying."

"How many?"

"Too many."

The phone rang. Tom Hall had both kinds of news. Dillon was a good man, and he readily committed a helicopter and rescue team to get Joe Loon out. But the weather prevented immediate action; the snowstorm had the area socked in good, and it looked like it would snow until nightfall. So they were planning to be in the air at dawn the next day if the sky was clear as expected.

Tom Hall promised to continue to monitor the situation regularly, to keep Brian informed, and to establish direct radio contact between the pilot and the dam operators.

Simon shared the news with the two white men.

"There's a spot on the other side of the dam where a helicopter could land."

"I will need help getting my grandfather to the dam."

"We have to stay here, but there will be a rescue team with the helicopter."

Simon stood as the idea occurred to him.

"The pilot will break the ice."

"Break the ice?"

"The top layer of ice. We will release the Northern Lights. No more deer or moose will fall to die when the top ice is gone. When the top ice is gone, the helicopter can land on the solid ice near shore where my grandfather will be waiting."

"So how do we break all that ice?"

"The pilot will use the helicopter."

Simon finished fixing the binding on his snowshoe with a bit of leather cord one of the white men found for him and was preparing to head back to his grandfather to care for him and tell him of the rescue plan.

Simon said goodbye and gave his thanks, then stepped outside into the heavy snowfall.

"Hold on a minute. I know where there are some extra blankets."

The white man returned with one folded blanket under his arm while he was folding the second. He handed them to Simon, who held them to his chest as he headed out to return to Joe Loon.

After he was out of sight from the two white men Simon unfolded one of the blankets and wrapped it around him as he walked along the shore between the trees and over the snow.

He was confident the repaired binding would hold.

Before long, it stopped snowing.

He felt he was making good time, but he didn't know this place, the shoreline wasn't familiar, and the day's hard snow made it less so, drifted here, piled on rocks, bending small firs with boughs holding full loads, and it was so very bright in the sun. Once Simon could no longer see the dam behind him as a measure of his progress he grew uncertain of where he was in his return to the shelter.

When he guessed he might be near enough he called out to Joe Loon, sending his shout up the shoreline through the trees. Then he stepped out on the ice and called out over the lake. There was no reply. It wasn't until he walked on much further and called the fourth time that he heard Joe Loon's voice in reply, though still at a distance.

The sun was descending, less than an hour of dusky daylight remained. There was barely any wind. Simon trudged on until he could see a faint wisp of smoke floating out over the lake up ahead from Joe Loon's fire, and he walked as fast as he could in the snow calling again.

"Grandfather."

"I am here."

When Simon could smell the smoke he began to speak of what was important.

"Big Brian is sending a helicopter in the morning."

Simon stepped past two more trees for a full view of the shelter and of his grandfather. He could see the snow walls were taller, and when he approached he saw his grandfather sat on a full cushion of pine boughs. The fire pit was partly framed with stones. All around the outside of the shelter the snow was flattened by his grandfather scooting along or dug up to find fire wood and stone. Simon smiled as he entered and found a second cushion of pine boughs for him. He took off his snowshoes, sat down preparing to tell his grandfather about his trip to the dam, but Joe Loon spoke first.

"You must tell the helicopter pilot to break all the false ice before he takes us away. He must release the death."

"Yes, Grandfather. That is what we will do."

Simon removed one of the blankets he'd wrapped over his shoulders to hand it to his grandfather.

"Where did you get those blankets?"

"From the white man. He gave them to me."

❄ ❄ ❄

When Kevin returned to the farmhouse Maureen was fixing an evening meal from the supplies he brought earlier. He sat down and began to share the new information he'd retrieved. She interrupted.

"Stop. You're worn to your core. Let's decide we won't lose the fight tonight if you allow yourself one even' of peace and quiet."

Kevin took Maureen's hand as his shoulders slumped.

"Thanks Lady Girl. You lead, and I'll do as told. I'm going to eat, and I'm going to bed."

"I have an idea, for a quick thrust at Stormont…" he perked up "…but as I say, the fight'll be waitin' in the mornin'."

"Yes, it will."

"Take rest now; I'll wake you when supper is ready."

He sat quietly, closed his eyes, and fell asleep.

Simon returned with another load of wood. He added it to the large stack he had already collected, slipped off his snowshoes, built the fire's blaze, then sat down next to Joe Loon at the fireside.

On the other side of his grandfather sat Grandmother and Young Sister.

Joe Loon told Simon to build a larger fire than usual since they expected this was their last night, and because this fire wasn't just to keep them warm. It had a special function.

Folded in front of Joe Loon were the two blankets Simon brought back from the dam.

"Many men from my grandfather's village went to work in the gold mines. The white man who worked there gave my grandfather many good things. The big pot Nokomis uses when we make Anishinaabe Ziinzibakwad, this pot was given to my grandfather by the white man who worked these mines. This is why we know the white man of the mines were not trying to kill our people when they gave us the pox blankets."

Grandmother and Young Sister began to pray.

Simon added more wood and fanned the flames.

"So many of our people died from the pox blankets. When you see their names on the Ancestor's Wall you cry for those who died. Then you cry for those who lived."

Simon picked up the top blanket and fed it into the blaze, standing over the fire using a stick to nudge the blankets into the flames to effectively consume the blanket, reducing it to a rough ash and pieces of scorched wool.

Grandmother and Young Sister continued their prayer. Joe Loon sat quietly, his eyes closed, listening for the ancestors.

As Simon fed the second blanket to the flames he spoke to his grandfather.

"When the white man built this dam, they did not mean to

harm our people or our brothers. But we must always be careful around them. It means giving up more of our forests to the white man, but to be safe we must never come back here again."

❉ ❉ ❉

Maureen was finishing cleaning up after supper and Kevin sat at the table sipping the cup of tea she fixed for him. She turned and toweled her hands.

"Where's the nearest telephone box?"

"There's one two kilometers towards town, at the cross roads with the first petrol station."

"I've got to call Brian."

"There is one thing you do need to know."

"What's that?"

"I've been able to confirm it. We have an infiltrator that we didn't know about."

"I figured that out already."

"We think it's the Armagh brigade, but we're not certain."

"Could it be one of yours?"

"I think all my lads are true."

"But you're not sure."

"I've been wrong about other things, but never about that... No, I'm not sure. As of this moment I'm not sure about anyone."

The look they shared was a new one for them. It was the first time Maureen didn't see the man promising to keep her safe. And he knew she saw it. "I just wanted you to factor that into your scheme. I'll be asleep when you get back from your call."

"Have a good rest."

❉ ❉ ❉

Once again, Brian and the others were in the hotel diner when Maureen called, but this time the hotel manager sent a clerk to track them down. Brian picked up Grace and followed the clerk to the front desk; they forwarded the call to a lobby telephone.

Brian had Grace answer it.

"When are you coming home?"

"Oh, my Gracie girl. I miss you so much. Are you havin' fun with Lil' Stevie in the hotel?"

"I'm having lots of fun. We saw a gorilla. And we went to this other place, it was like a zoo for fish, where they have different fishes from around the world in big glass cages. And we got to ride on a train that drives up in the sky. I miss you. When are you coming home?"

"Soon sweetheart, soon. Is Mary takin' good care of you?"

"Yes."

"Is Da there?"

"He's here next to me. Do you want to talk to him?"

"Yes, please."

Brian took the phone from his daughter.

"Hello."

"Brian, honey, I'm sorry I haven't called like I promised."

Brian's voice was cold, hard. "I'm sure you have good reasons."

"You got my message I called yesterday?"

"I got the message."

"You're angry."

"I can't tell you how I feel right now."

"I just got so busy, attendin' to birthdays an' plannin' communion parties."

"Sure."

Brian looked up and saw that Dutch and the others were coming his way.

"Say goodbye to Gracie, an' then you an' I can talk."

He handed the phone back to his daughter.

"I want you to come home right now."

"Oh, Gracie girl, I wish I could. I'll be home very soon though, and I will hold you, hold you, hold you."

"I love you."

"I love you."

Brian waited until Grace was gone with the group.

"I was scared, Maureen. I thought somethin' must have happened to you. Why else wouldn't you call your daughter for nearly four days."

"I think it was more like two an' a half—"

"You don't want to play that game with me right now."

"What game?"

"Where you're always right an' happy to point out where I'm wrong."

"I don't want to play any games with you Brian."

"Well, do you have anythin' you want to ask me, or tell me?"

"The shows are goin' well?"

"Yes."

"Have you taken Dutch to our blues clubs yet?"

"We are plannin' on doin' that tonight."

"Brian, my time is runnin' out. I'm callin' from a public phone box and have but a minute or so left. Please say somethin' nice to me."

"As soon as you return."

"Brian, please."

"I love you, but I feel abandoned by you right now, so I'm afraid that's the best I can give you."

"I'll get home as soon as I can."

"Alright then. Thanks for callin'. Say hi to your mum."

"I will."

"An' to Kevin."

"Kevin? I don't expect to see him, but, sure, if I do, I'll tell him you asked about him."

"Call me when you know your plans for comin' home. Goodbye."

❅ ❅ ❅

It was another cloudless night. Joe Loon slept. Simon was tending the fire; they had allowed it to burn down to a warming fire. Grandmother and Young Sister sat at the fire as Simon stirred the flames and sent a twisting flurry of sparks dancing.

Above and near the horizon, as the night sky cleared, the Northern Lights began to shimmer. Simon was watching the show when the sound surprised him. It was a sound he had never heard before, coming from the lake, or across the lake. There was a sucking whoosh followed by a crash. He stood, but it was too dark to see anything on the lake. He heard it again, and much later it happened one more time.

He slept much of the night, waking when Grandmother stirred him to build the fire.

Brian sat in a chair in his hotel room, Dutch sat in another, and Mary Fobister stood by the bathroom door, the children bathing in the tub together behind her. Brian told them the latest news about Joe Loon and Simon, and of the scheduled rescue for the next morning. He was trying to convince Mary they should stick with their original plan for the evening, to go hear some great blues music, and Dutch was helping, but Mary shook her head no as she wiped her hands on a bath towel.

"I am thinking of Simon and Joe Loon all of the time. I will stay here."

"You will be thinkin' about them if you stay here. But not if you come with us."

"I do not wish to celebrate when they are cold and hungry."

"You bring 'em neither warmth nor nourishment by stayin' in tonight."

"Yes. I do. I keep them in my prayers. They feel this. When I keep them in my heart, they know this. It keeps them warm. This is what my people believe, and I believe this to be so."

Brian nodded. "My people believe this, too, yeah. Sometimes we need some remindin'." Then he asked if she would lead them in a prayer right then, for a safe night and an early rescue. They stood just outside the bathroom door. Dutch closed his eyes, Brian bowed his head, and Mary lifted hers up as she spoke the language the Great Creator gave to the Original People, who gave it to her ancestors.

"Great Father. I have traveled far from the place of your people, but you will know the voice of Brown Wren. I stand in the white man's great city of mountain shelters. In this noisy place please hear me speak to you, here in this place called Che Kowago."

Little Stevie looked up from the bath at the sound of prayer in his mother's voice, and he saw them standing there. He touched Grace O'Malley's shoulder for her attention. They both leaned forward, their chins resting on their hands resting on the side of the tub, her naked white body and his naked brown one pressed together side by side, for warmth, for touch, and they watched together; Little Stevie listened to the prayer and Grace O'Malley listened to the sounds and for any words she might know.

"I ask Great Father to look after Joe Loon and Simon. Joe Loon has lived in your forests for many years. He shows you great honor every day." Grace stood, and Little Stevie stood with her, and they held hands, and watched. "He respects the Ancestors. He honors the spirits of all the Animals of the forest. He protects the River every day. You see him teach the love of your forest and your River to his grandson. Please make the night a peaceful one for all of your children. Please make the morning clear and calm for all of your children. Please bring Joe Loon and his grandson safely back to his people."

When it was clear she had finished Brian crossed himself and whispered the Trinity, Amen, and Dutch sat on the edge of the bed, silently considering what else he might do to assure the morning's rescue. Mary had tossed the towel on a chair before they prayed; she retrieved it and returned to the bathroom to get the children out of the tub.

While she dressed them in their pajamas, Brian was able, finally, to convince her to at least come with them for the first part of the evening, and they called the switchboard to send up the babysitter.

Dutch, Brian, and Mary sat at a table near the stage of the blues club on Chicago's South Side that Brian and Maureen visited every night they were in Chicago once they discovered it. Willie Smith was fronting his own band, playing the harmonica and singing "If you don' start believin', when I tell ya I am leavin', one day you're gonna wake up... an' I'll be gone" backed by bass, electric guitar, and drums.

Dutch leaned forward, his fingers in his white hair, a great smile on his face. Brian sat back in his chair, hands folded behind his head, his eyes closed. Mary sat between them, sipping her ginger ale through a straw as she studied the exotic setting. She had seen a black man before, during one of her infrequent trips to Kenora, but only that one time, and he was all by himself. This room was filled with black men, and black women, and she was entranced by their beauty.

And she had never before sipped a drink through a straw.

Brian rocked forward until his chair sat on all four legs and edged a bit closer to Mary as the song was winding to a close, then spoke when the music stopped.

"What'a you say to that?"

She nodded approval and smiled.

"Think the village would enjoy it?"

She nodded again and her smile grew when she imagined her family and friends from her village there with her.

"We're flyin' back first thing in the mornin'. So if our help is needed there hain't a thing we can do to get there sooner. If you wanted to, you could relax an' enjoy the music."

She nodded a third time. "But if I decide to go you will have someone take me back to the hotel and the children?"

"Whenever you say so, yeah."

Dutch joined the conversation.

"And since I'm flying tomorrow I won't want to stay real late anyway."

Mary nodded one more time.

"There is magic in this music. Much magic. It is very loud and that makes it hard for me to hear all the magic. But there is much magic."

"Last year when Maureen an' I were here we learned how natives to this place, I mean the regulars here, how they dance to it. They called it the Slow Drag."

"I would like to dance to this music."

Brian was out on the dance floor doing the Slow Drag with the club owner's wife; the club owner and his wife taught the step to him and Maureen on their second trip there.

Dutch sat at the table, alone, sipping the one beer he allowed himself whenever he had an early morning flight, enjoying the music.

In a far corner of the club, behind a half wall that blocked much of the room and absorbed some of the loudness from the music, Mary Fobister of the Loon and Sturgeon clans, was dancing; it had started out as a traditional Ojibway dance step, though this music's powerful back beat was transforming it into something else, into something she'd never danced before. Two regulars, black women who had been leaning on a wall far enough away from the music so that they could talk, stopped complaining about their boyfriends, and watched Mary and her moves. They began to bob and weave their shoulders and heads, feeling what Mary was feeling, and smiling their support for it when she saw them.

Maureen awoke in the early dawn and looked in to discover Kevin's bed empty, then found his car was gone. She made herself tea and bottled it, wrapped some food left over from supper, collected her blanket and all her papers, and headed out to the Proleek Dolmen again, just as the sun was rising, just as the day was awakening.

She had her notebook open and was reviewing her notes for the Stormont mission and checking on the questions that needed answers when she heard a call in the wind, and the sound was joyous. She tucked her notebook under the blanket as a boy and a girl, she in her late teens, the boy in his early twenties, both of them dressed as service staff of the nearby hotel, crested a rise and headed for the Dolmen.

They were surprised for a moment to find Maureen there and said good morning but were happy to then ignore her and stand together on the opposite side of the tomb, hidden from Maureen's view. Their sounds were sweet, hers and his.

In a moment Maureen's attention was attracted by a small stone skipping across the top of the dolmen's capstone, bouncing off one of the other stones before it fell to the ground accompanied by a cry of dismay from the girl. A few moments later another stone, tossed with more arc, landed on the capstone and bounced and bounced and slid to the ground, and this time the girl called out her confidence in "My Ryan's" next try.

And the next toss was successful, as the stone hit two others and came to rest between them, joining the others atop the capstone, and the boy and girl laughed together. She led him boldly by the hand around the tomb towards Maureen, and they were both smiling. She let go of his hand as she walked up to the edge of the blanket.

"You're our witness."

Maureen smiled at their delight.

"Gladly so, but what exactly have I just witnessed?"

"The stone Ryan tossed stayed a'top of the Giant's Load."

"Yes, then I'm a witness, though I never heard it called the Giant's Load."

Ryan spoke. "S'what the Proddies round here call it, yeah." And he tried to sneak a tickle to his girlfriend's side as he said, "Proddies."

"That's 'cause it was a Proddie who brought it here, the great Scottish giant Parrah Boug MacShagean himself carried the capstone over his shoulder you see, from his homeland."

"Yeah so, an' the Irish he found here knew there was plenty a' stones all around, no need to be importin' 'em from Scotland." Again, the boy's joke gave him permission to touch her.

Maureen smiled at them.

"Tell me Ryan, why'd you toss your stones so?"

"If two sweethearts stand together and toss a stone that lands on top of the Giant's Load and it stays there, if it don't fall off, legend says they'll be married inside of a year."

"An' that's your intent?"

The girl answered. "Our intentions and our plans and our hopes and our prayers."

"An' a source of constant sorrow?"

"Why would you say such a thing?"

"I'm right in seein' you're one an' you're the other?"

The girl laughed.

"You mean my Ryan a Catholic and myself a Proddie?"

"That's what I'm guessin' by your carryin' on."

Ryan laughed.

"You're right 'cept you're wrong. I'm the Proddie an' she's the follower of the Holy Roman Faith, the One True Church, Amen." He treated this as another tease, and tickled her delight. Maureen let them enjoy the moment before she asked, "An' so now you be my witnesses an' tell me what sort of sorrows come your way in these parts from proclaimin' your love is more important than which Jesus is the best Jesus an' God damn the others."

The girl answered.

"All our friends only marry within their own faith, that's true. But we both know of a mixed marriage that is makin' a go."

"It's simple. Do the parents accept? Mine accept, no problem."

"And mine… well just look at my Ryan and tell me who wouldn't love him?"

"An' your children?"

The lovers turned to each other, and he questioned her with his look. She nodded yes as she said, "Tell her. Let me hear you say it."

"Just yesterday you said keep the secret still."

"There's no one she can tell… We're going to get married and then we're going to America. To Boston. Ryan's uncle moved there ten years ago. It won't make a difference there what we do about raising our children in which ever faith that we decide."

"Oh honey, it makes a difference everywhere. But you got a far better chance of it in Boston, I have to agree to that."

The couple was eager to get on with whatever their love drove them to next, and they departed as delighted as when they arrived. Maureen listened to the joy of their voices from the other side of the Giant's Load for another few minutes and then smiled to see how their bodies played off each other through their long journey to the top of the ridge.

She opened her notebook. She found the list she had started on the plane over, a list she ignored once she arrived. It was the list of reasons why she should simply visit her mother for her birthday and attend the Holy Communion of her niece, and then return to Kenora as soon as she could.

Seeing the list made her angry, and she ripped it from the notebook, and burned it.

Then she began ripping one page after another, pages with notes about the Stormont raid and questions about Kevin's brigade, and one at a time she twisted them into wicks, and she burned them all.

A small flock of warblers were working their way along the edge of the grove from her left, slowly leap frogging each other in the branches until they were nearly overhead, briefly, before hopping and flitting and jumping their way, as first one then the others darted across the open space to a nearby smaller grove, away from the smoke, in the full morning sun, and the source of the early morning's most vibrant bird song.

Maureen saw none of this as she continued burning all the papers she had. When she was finished she spread any remaining ashes around the base of the tomb.

※ ※ ※

Kevin was waiting when Maureen returned mid-morning.

"You must leave Ireland as soon as you can Lady Girl."

Maureen's smile covered her surprise at Kevin's words.

"That's what I was just now decidin', Kevin."

"I mean now. Fast. It seems the gentleman who first took your call is suspected of bleeding Orange."

"Tell me what's happenin' then."

"I don't have a specific warning, but the breach in our ranks seems greater than any of us suspected. You need to get in your car right now and get to the airport as fast as you can."

"I've got to see Mum first. Then I'll go."

"I'm not sure that is the wise course."

"I'm thinkin' Kev, because of what I've done, all I've done now... that I may never come back." The full weight of that hadn't occurred to her before. "So I'm goin' to visit her, an' tell her, an' see if she will come with me. Then we'll leave."

"I insist you go now."

"You can't insist anythin'."

"Then move quickly and carefully."

"An' you, Kevin Coogan. Why not come with us?"

"Live with you and Brian and your Indians?"

"You were always quick to see it as Eden."

"To live with you in Eden."

"The fishin' camp is growin' like blazes, which means the business side of things keeps gettin' to be more an' more an' Bri has little interest in that, in the business side of things, he'd be the first to agree. An' then the bush plane business is startin' to come back again after all the business we lost, an' Dutch has said countless times he'd like to go back to flyin' full-time if we could find someone to run NOA."

"And what would I know about running an airline?"

"We're makin' all this up as we go along, Kevin. Brian an' I don't know how to run a bush plane airline or a fishin' camp an' so we just keep makin' it up… even better I'll bet you'd figure out lots of ways to help us manage our relationships with the pulp mill operators an' the dam builders an' all the rest who want to spoil our Eden."

"It does occur to me at times that your love is more wisely invested than my own. You've got Brian and Grace, your Indians… your Heaven on Earth. And I've got this fight here in front of me."

"Your love needs to be your life. This fight'll be your death."

Kevin smiled at the truth of that.

"I wish you wouldn't cross back into the North."

"I've got to see Mum."

"Yes, I see."

They embraced.

"Sorry Kev."

"Don't be."

"This could be the last time I see you."

"Who knows? I showed up once unexpected; I just might surprise you and Brian again."

"I pray to God that be so."

She stepped away, then turned back.

"You know I've always trusted you. An' that I've always loved you?"

"Be safe Lady Girl."

❄ ❄ ❄

Maureen drove her rented car back north on the road from Dundalk to Dungannon. The roadblock was still there from two days before. There were only half as many men, but she recognized the senior officer and he was looking for her. He waved her over.

"It's the light of day, mam, and anyone crossing the border in your pattern is suspect, every solicitor agrees that's reasonable."

"If I'm suspected of thinkin' that the lot of ya' disgrace this land you're standin' upon, I'm guilty."

"Get out of the automobile and stand next to that constable there. If you would like a cup of tea, let him know. He'll be happy to fetch it for you."

"The damage to the car hain't felt by me if you decide to tear it up lookin.'"

"Looking for what?"

She stepped out of the car, and opened her handbag, offering it to the officer to examine.

"Lookin' to terrorize anyone who speaks of the murderous crimes you an' your sort has perpetrated against the true Irish for four centuries now."

The officer examined her bag then handed it back to her, and she stepped out of the way of the approaching uniformed men.

"I'm sayin' it's a hired car, yeah, an' I'll make sure to give 'em your name as the one responsible for any damage done to it."

The officer rubbed his hands, and turned to the men who were waiting to do damage to the car.

"Give it the best search you can without costing the Crown."

"Without costin' the Crown? You talk that way? You actually say 'the Crown?' "

"Get her some tea. Maybe that'll shut her up."

Maureen waited until the constable left her to get the tea before she turned just a bit and slipped her pistol from her sleeve into her handbag.

As the men gave the hired car a thorough search, inside and out, under every space, within every opening, deeply probing the upholstery—without damaging it—she recited for them the lyrics of the song of Roddy McCorley at Toome Bridge.

She started softly, so only those closest could hear.

"See the fleet-footed host a' men, who march with faces drawn,
From farmstead an' from fishers' cot, along the banks of Ban;
They come with vengeance in their eyes. Too late! Too late are they,
For young Roddy McCorley goes to die on the bridge a' Toome today."

Then she got louder.

"Ireland, Mother Ireland, you love them still the best
Those fearless brave who fightin' fall upon your hapless breast,
But never a one of all your dead more bravely fell in fray,
Than he who marches to his fate on the bridge of Toome today.
Up the narrow street he stepped, smilin' proud an' young.
About the hemp-rope on his neck his golden ringlets clung..."

She was loud enough now all could hear her, and she continued though the men shouted out to stop.

"…There's not a tear in his blue eyes, fearless an' brave are they,

As young Roddy McCorley goes to die on the bridge a' Toome today.

When last this narrow street he trod, his shinin' pike in hand

Behind him marched, in grim array, an earnest stalwart band.

To Antrim town! To Antrim town! He led them to the fray,

But young Roddy McCorley goes to die on the bridge a' Toome today.

His grey coat an' its sash a' green were brave an' stainless then,

A banner flashed beneath the sun an' o'er the marchin' men;

His coat has many a rent this noon, his sash is torn away,

An' Roddy McCorley goes to die on the bridge of Toome today…"

The men trying to shout her down had abandoned their search of the car and their language was menacing, but she stared at the commanding officer and looked him in the eyes and continued as another car pulled up, deflating the anger of the men a bit as the car was quickly waved through. The officer matched Maureen's gaze as he walked towards her.

"…Oh, how his pike flashed in the sun! Then found a foeman's heart,

Through furious fight, an' heavy odds he bore a true man's part

An' many a red-coat bit the dust before his keen pike-play,

But Roddy McCorley goes to die on the bridge a' Toome today…"

The officer took her arm and pulled her towards her car, for the men had completed their search.

"…young Roddy McCorley goes to die on the bridge a' Toome today."

She tossed her handbag into the car in the same motion she raised her arms out to the side for a body search.

"If you had any decency at all you'd have a female officer for this… Oh that's right, you're British."

The officer searched her body, first carefully but then carelessly.

"I pity your wife."

The officer pushed her into her car.

"Get out of here."

Maureen drove away, watching the officer in the mirror as long as she could.

When she was out of sight, the officer reached for the radio.

"London Bomber Six just passed. Driving north towards Dungannon in a hired Ford Prefect, white, license plate Alpha Romeo Romeo One Zero Three. She was wearing a green coat. We searched her and her car closely. It appears she is not armed."

As soon as there was light Simon climbed up on top of the boulder, first to check the sky—he found it clear as far as he could see—and then he studied the lake ice. He found that a large portion of the ice ceiling had collapsed near the far shore. He turned to his grandfather to tell him the good news.

"The sound I heard last night, I think it was some of the top ice collapsing."

"The top ice has fallen in?"

"Not all of it. A large section near the far shore. And the hole where we fell in looks like it might be bigger."

They stoked their fire and ate more freely from their food stores.

Simon left the shelter for the shore using a stone and a hand axe to break away the ice that covered the ground and stumps between the ice floor and ceiling to create a path up the steep incline. Standing on the ice floor he looked out towards the middle of the lake and through the swirling lights he could see a moose laying still, his legs folded under, his head tucked, as if asleep. He walked towards it and didn't need to get too close before determining it was dead.

Simon had just finished his path from the shelter to the ice when he heard the helicopter in the distance. By the time he climbed back out Joe Loon had tossed some of the pine boughs on the fire to create a heavy smoke signal. Simon mounted the boulder again to watch the helicopter work its way from the dam along the shore, coming closer and closer until the pilot spotted them and waved. When Simon waved back, the pilot gave him thumbs up before he veered back out over the ice.

"He is going to break the ice to land."

"Help me stand so I can see."

Simon jumped down from the boulder to help Joe Loon lean against it, then he pulled back a large spruce bough so they could watch as the pilot of the Bell 47 hovered over the ice ceiling, slowly lowering the craft, his large pontoons just a foot or so over the ice, his blades kicking up a broad bowl of swirling snow. Then the pilot descended for a hard landing on the ice ceiling and a large section of it gave way as the helicopter rose quickly and again hovered a few feet above so the pilot could survey the results. They watched as the pilot worked his way along the edge of the first hole he'd made, bouncing his large pontoons on the ice ceiling, knocking more and more of it down, the helicopter surrounded by dancing snow clouds.

When the pilot determined he had knocked down enough of the ice all along the shore to land he lowered the copter until the pontoons set down on the solid floor ice, and the blades slowed, then stopped. The pilot and a man carrying a stretcher stepped out and waved and slid along the ice to the shore. Simon met them there.

"Sorry we couldn't get you out last night. It was snowing too hard."

Simon showed them the path he made and they climbed out.

"So who's hurt?"

"My grandfather. Both of his legs are injured. Our shelter is just behind that big rock."

He led them to the shelter and they found Joe Loon, sitting back again.

"You guys fell, what, that had to be nearly twenty feet, eh? You think you got any broken bones?"

"Grandfather doesn't speak English. His right ankle may be broken. His left knee will not bend without a great pain. He does not say this but I am sure it hurts all the time."

They unfolded the stretcher and supported Joe Loon as he settled on it.

"And you fell through as well?"

"Yes, we were walking together."

"You're lucky you didn't get hurt."

"I fell on top of my bag. It was under me when I landed."

"The nearest hospital is in Kenora and that'll take almost two hours. We'll have to get refueled."

Simon translated the pilot's words for his grandfather.

"Tell the pilot he must take me to Grassy Narrows."

"You cannot take Grandfather to the hospital in Kenora."

"Why not?"

"They do not care for us there."

"What do you mean?"

"The hospital in Kenora is for the white man. Not for the Indian."

"Are you sure?"

"My uncle was turned away when he had an injury. So was Tommy Keewatin."

"Then where do we take him?"

"You must take us back to Grassy Narrows."

"Your grandfather needs to be seen by a doctor."

"There is a doctor who comes to visit us once a month. But he will come sooner when we radio him to tell him he is needed."

"You can radio him from the helicopter and maybe he can meet us there."

They strapped Joe Loon onto the stretcher and slowly worked their way down to the ice floor. He was loaded in the helicopter, sitting up on the stretcher just before takeoff.

"You must tell the pilot to break the rest of the ice."

Simon called up to the pilot.

"You must break the ice ceiling."

"What's that?"

"You must break the ice ceiling. All of it."

"Look, I'm not exactly sure how far it is to the Reserve, I need to get more fuel, and I got a long day ahead of me as it is."

"You saw the dead moose. He fell through the ice and was trapped in between. There are many animals trapped down here. They die when they cannot get out."

"I'm sorry, but we'd have to bounce up and down on this ice all day to get it all knocked down."

Simon told his grandfather as the helicopter lifted off, rising slowly until it cleared the ice ceiling. A smile came to Joe Loon's face.

"Tell him to be a skipping stone."

Simon knew exactly what his grandfather meant.

"It will be fun. Fly to far end of the River's lake then bounce your way back to the dam, bounce hard..." Simon surveyed quickly. "...five times and by the fifth bounce all the ice will fall."

The pilot pictured it, and shook his head as he described it to his crewmate. They nodded, they smiled, and the helicopter set off to the south end of the long narrow River valley lake. The pilot conferred again with his crewmate, then turned to Simon. "I think it will take six bounces, we'll give it our best shot, but one way or another, we are on our way."

Simon nodded his understanding as he translated for his grandfather.

The pilot turned when he reached the far edge of the lake, turned, and flew over the ice towards the dam and after a few moments he dove down hard, bouncing the pontoons against the ice ceiling and rising fast the instant the impact was made, and Simon saw the impact was effective, looking back to see the hole was large and growing larger when the helicopter again dove down hard, and again knocked a hole, and then sped on and dove for another hole, and this third one Simon thought was much larger, much faster, and then the fourth hole reached out to the hole Joe Loon and Simon made when they fell through and now a great section gave away; the pilot bounced twice more and elevated for one look at the work and saw they'd been effective, pieces were still collapsing, but much of the top ice had fallen in, a raggedy sharp toothed grin of a River valley left behind.

❋ ❋ ❋

Maureen knew a car was following her out of Dungannon as she drove northwest to Pomeroy; the tail made no effort at hiding himself, making her anxious. She stopped at the small village's phone box and the car passed by, then pulled over just ahead and waited. She entered the phone box, pistol in hand though out of sight, and called the emergency number for Kevin, but no one answered.

She called the townhouse in Kenora. No one answered.

To buy a few moments and to make her tail think about it, she pretended to talk on the phone. As she pantomimed her end of the conversation, she wondered if she should walk up to the man in the car to ask what he was doing, prepared to shoot him.

She considered it self-defense.

She got back in her car and drove past the tail car; it pulled right out onto the road, and followed a steady constant ten car lengths behind.

She drove on through the quiet countryside. If she sped up, so did the tail car. If she slowed down, the car behind her did too.

She was followed through the tiny village of Carrickmore, past the RUC barracks there, and on west towards a wide River valley. The car stayed right on her tail, in clear sight, ten car lengths behind.

The road crested a rise and she looked down at the broad shallow bowl of a valley, with a three arch stone bridge carrying the road over the River. She pictured the next village was Six Mile Cross, three or four miles on the other side of the bridge.

A car was parked near the bridge, and that concerned her; she noticed the fly fisherman wading the River just below the bridge.

She checked the car behind her, keeping its close measure.

She focused on the fisherman. Before she could identify the personal details of him she could see how he handled his fly rod. By his second cast she knew he was a fisherman, and that brought some relief.

She slowed as she drew near the bridge, taking in every detail of the scene laid out in front of her; the car behind her kept the distance constant.

Maureen decided to park next to the fisherman's car and walk down to the River; she looked for a spot to pull over but slammed on the brakes when the head and shoulders of a man popped up behind the steering wheel of the parked car. She hadn't noticed until then that this car's engine was running, and she was angry at herself when the driver stepped on the accelerator, turned hard back up onto the road, and blocked the bridge with his car.

Maureen stopped, twenty yards from the bridge. She took a

deep breath, then another, to empty her emotions, to reset herself, for she knew that whatever happened next, she had to be at her best, and she began to look for options and consider their odds.

The fisherman was wading quickly towards shore while she reached into her bag.

The tail car stopped, ten car lengths behind hers.

She pulled her pistol from her bag. Its cylinder held five rounds; she reminded herself one was spent.

The driver of the car at the bridge was getting out.

The fisherman was climbing the River's bank.

The driver of the car behind opened his door.

She hadn't seen any guns, so far. She expected to.

Maureen slipped off the pistol's safety. She looked for other cars on both horizons, but none were coming. The fisherman was climbing from the River to the road, the driver in front of her removed his pistol from his coat, and her quick look over her shoulder told her the driver behind her was out of his car carrying a Sten machine gun.

Maureen figured the man with the Sten as the first target; as long as the fisherman appeared unarmed, he would be the final target. She slipped the pistol into the sleeve loop, then nodded to show she would roll down the window.

The fisherman stepped onto the road. She was practiced at disarming, and she called out to him.

"I've heard of anglers goin' to great lengths to protect a favorite stretch of water..."

The fisherman worked hard to keep from laughing; the man with the Sten couldn't help himself. She saw it was a good moment to make a move but it had come too soon, she wasn't ready.

For one thing, each of the men were still too far; the snub nose made her pistol a short range weapon, even in her expert hand.

The man at the bridge knew he had to take control, so he waved his pistol in the air.

"Keep your hands where we can see them, right."

"You don't need a gun to have a conversation with a Canadian tourist."

"You're Maureen O'Toole."

"I'm Maureen Burke. I've got an Ontario driver's license here says so."

The fisherman joined the man at the bridge and stood close by his side. She appreciated they were organizing her targets for her. She pictured a surprise move to take out the machine gun behind her—now she'd aim for the man's chest, the largest one shot kill target—and then she'd duck and spin and…

"Open the door and get out of the car."

"You don't need to be wavin' that around so. You don't need it at all is what I'm sayin'."

Maureen got out, leaving the door open, and stood behind it.

"Close the door and step away from the car."

She did, and at the same time she turned enough so the man behind her wasn't anymore, and she also took a full step closer to him, a move hidden in her turn; now the man with the Sten was nearly in range.

She reminded herself she couldn't afford to miss.

"I know I am looking at Maureen O'Toole, born in Derry to Donovan and Mary O'Toole."

"Ah then, you introduce the more important question now don't you, an' that is this. Do you know who Donovan O'Toole was?"

"Shut up. I know that when you were nineteen, that on two occasions, the first in January 1939, the second in June, you smuggled the mines and gelignite to your terrorist friends in London who built the bombs that killed British citizens and destroyed British property."

The fisherman spoke.

"That means Donovan O'Toole should be damned for bringing a soul as black as yours into the world."

She still didn't like her position so she tried to buy some more time.

"All you need to know about Donovan O'Toole was he was a true Irishman who believed the Brits have no right to ever tell a true Irishman how he can live in his own land. For that basic belief of Donovan O'Toole a Black n' Tan scum shot him dead an' forced his family to watch." She smiled thinking of what she had done to avenge her da's murder and wondered if she should she confess it now; perhaps it would upset their balance.

She decided it wasn't the right time. The two men near the bridge were still too far. One against three—she wasn't *sure* the fisherman wasn't armed—and just four bullets, her only chance was to make every shot a killing shot.

The driver at the bridge called out to the man with the Sten.

"Your father was a Black n' Tan, wasn't he?"

"That's right. He was a hero."

Maureen finished her turn to stand sideways to the men and spoke to them all, the two men near the bridge to her left, the man with the Sten to her right.

"I'll tell a story about Black n' Tan heroes, yeah."

"If you're buying time for someone to come along, we got an RUC road block behind you, a road repair block ahead."

"So I can take my time an' tell you all about the Black n' Tan heroes who took Donovan O'Toole from his bed one night, tied his hands behind his back—" She put her hands behind her back and slipped the pistol into her right hand, and as long as she told the story she could keep her hands and pistol hidden, and ready, behind her. "—an' then they beat him. An' you can only understand the heroic consequences of this story if you linger for a moment on the sequence of those events. They tied him up, then they beat him. I know because I was there. That's the stuff of Black n' Tan heroes right there. Ya' sing songs in your British pubs celebratin' that, do ya?"

The man at the bridge started walking towards Maureen. In a few more steps he'd be close enough and that would put two of them in her practiced range; there was still no evidence the fisherman was armed.

"Time for you to shut up, and let's talk about what happens next."

"Oh I know what happens next, so answer this for me before you send me on my way. How many true Irish did a Black n' Tan have to kill to be a hero?"

He quickened his step a bit, watching her carefully, waiting for her move; she wanted him to come closer and as long as his gun was at his side she let him.

"For you see, after they beat him to the ground they made him get to his knees." Maureen got down on her knees, her hands still behind her, waiting for the man coming her way to take two more steps, her finger already on the trigger of her pistol; she was most accurate from a practiced kneeling position and she could assume it quickly.

The man before her stopped as she knelt and the man with the Sten came to the ready position and stepped behind her again, and Maureen knew he'd see her pistol so she had to act; she shifted her weight and just before she pulled the pistol from behind her back he did see it.

"She's got a gun!"

The man standing before Maureen raised his pistol when he saw her weight shift and the look in Maureen's face change, and aimed and fired twice before Maureen could get a shot off. The first bullet hit her in the chest and ripped through a lung, and the second tore a hole in her stomach. She dropped her gun as she fell back on the road.

The men approached her cautiously, guns ready. The man with the Sten picked up her pistol. Her eyes were open, and she was breathing, and she raised her head.

She was covered in blood and it ran from her mouth as she coughed up her words.

"I kill...who killed Dono...in Banbrid..."

She coughed and the blood was foamy, and she lay her head down on a pillow of thick black curls and her blue eyes went gray when she took her last breath.

This Man and Mathew Loon and all the spirits who gathered at this sacred place, where the funeral pyres burned, where Mathew Loon sacrificed himself to save the River, they changed their song. They still called to the spirits of this sacred place, and they called to a new spirit, that was also an old spirit.

They hadn't been able to raise the doctor over the helicopter's radio during the ride to Grassy Narrows, and the Hudson Bay Post was closed with the agent away for two days, so that radio would not be available to them to try again until four full days after the accident.

Joe Loon was lying on a pallet of blankets and furs as Naomi examined his injured legs again and softly rubbed an ointment on the injuries. The ankle was swollen and discolored, protected and held stable with a forest splint. The knee had been puffed up to nearly twice its normal size, but a lot of the swelling had subsided.

Naomi's touch was very gentle.

"I cannot walk until they heal."

"When the Hudson Bay Post opens again Simon will radio for the doctor."

Her touch was soothing.

"It is clear my ankle is broken. I do not know what is wrong with my knee."

Naomi stopped to pull the blanket back up over her husband, pressing her body close to his as she did.

"I am just glad my husband has returned to me."

"I am glad to be lying next to my wife in this world."

Naomi laid her head on his chest and began to rub his stomach.

"A good wife knows what will make her husband's pain go away."

Naomi reached down under the blanket and rubbed her husband softly.

"You have always been a good wife."

❄ ❄ ❄

The men decided to leave a false crime scene. The fisherman used Maureen's pistol to shoot her rental car, three times. Then he slipped the pistol under the front seat of the car.

"That'll keep 'em guessing."

They hid the rental car behind some thick bushes growing by the side of the River.

They wrapped Maureen in a tarp and loaded her in the trunk of the tail car, and they hid her body where no one would ever find it.

Chapter 9
BETWEEN WORLDS

THE FIRST PHONE CALL Brian made upon learning from his mother-in-law that Maureen was missing was to their attorney, alerting him. The second was a radio call to the Hudson Bay Post setting in motion the conversation he wanted to have with Albert about Mary joining him on this trip, to take care of Grace; he wanted his daughter with him, or close by with his family, while he searched for his wife; since his family were strangers to his daughter he hoped Mary could join them again.

Albert wondered if Big Brian shouldn't just go alone, suggesting they would take care of Grace at Grassy Narrows.

"I thought of that, an' thanks for offerin'. An' if she found out you made the offer she might be preferin' to stay there with her brothers an' sisters, sure. But Albert, I'm thinkin' of myself here, an' I'll feel better knowin' she's close by. Over."

"We will get Mary ready to travel with you. Over."

"Thanks Albert. Thanks for everything. Over."

"My brother. Joe Loon wants you to know he will be calling on all the spirits of this world and the next world and the world of Jesus the Christ to guide your journey to a happy ending. Over and out."

"Over and out."

Thirty hours after the phone call from Maureen's mother Brian exited the plane in Dublin, carrying his daughter in his arms, followed by Mary, expecting to find his cousin Eamon and his daughter Katie waiting for him, pleased his son Tommy was there as well. Katie was in her early twenties, Tommy his mid-twenties; as a fully ordained priest, the vestigial tab to his priest's collar was showing. Brian gave Grace a hug before he put her down and gestured to Katie. "There's your sister Katie. We've told you stories of Katie." Grace O'Malley reached back to take Mary's hand and led her to meet her sister.

Brian saw the immediate comfort between the Ojibway woman, the Irish woman, and his daughter, and wished Maureen was there to see it. When he joined Tommy standing with Eamon he noticed his son had a small travel bag with him.

"Any news while I was travelin'?"

"Sorry Coz, still nothin' but confusion about it. No one seems to know anythin' other than she's still missin.'"

"Thanks for takin' Gracie. You'll find Mary takes good care … Can I ask about Patrick?"

"Patrick wouldn't come."

"I understand… But he sent no word?"

"I'd be lyin' to you if I said so, sorry."

"Give him my regards."

Tommy raised his travel bag a bit. "I'm coming along with you. If you want some company and perhaps some help."

"I'm in need of your comfort an' of all the help I can get. Comin' over I was thinkin' I would need Maureen to help me find her… I can't believe she's missin'… Nothin' about her…"

Eamon and Katie followed by Grace O'Malley and Mary left for Cong. It would have been more convenient to have flown into the Shannon airport for his Cong relatives, but Brian wanted to retrace Maureen's steps as closely as he could; Maureen would have suggested that. So Tommy and Brian checked with each car hire service and found Maureen Burke had rented a white Ford Prefect; they noted the license plate, then hired their own car. They left Dublin on the road to Dundalk on their way to Derry.

They assumed Maureen would drive the most direct route; they plotted it and followed it, as she had. They would keep their eyes out from the start for anything that might be a sign that she was there.

With their attention directed, they spoke infrequently, and when they did it came in short bursts.

They were approaching the spot where Maureen was killed; Tommy was getting his first look at the bridge and the River when he said, "Whenever you say Kevin Coogan's name, you say it like you think he's done something wrong here. That this is his fault."

"I've never been sure what to think of that fella', but at this point, yeah, I *do* think he's involved in whatever's happenin' here."

"Then why would he call on her mum to check in on Maureen?"

"To make it look like he didn't have anythin' to do with it? That's what Maureen would say."

They drove much of the way in silence until Brian asked, "How *is* Patrick?"

"The same."

"Meanin'?"

"His spells are neither better nor worse. Sometimes he says he's dizzy. Sometimes he says he's faint. He says it's the electricity of his brain shorts out for a few seconds and he never knows quite how his body will react, that's his current best explanation. Two or three spells a week is what he tells me, and Katie says more often it's four or five."

"An' he still curses me."

"Once again he sees you in the center of a chaotic and violent scene takin' place. The way he puts it, I'm sorry, he says you wear violence as your mantle. Often he says it's your natural wake. But honestly he's told us not to mention you, because he doesn't want to think about you at all."

For a few moments Brian found his sadness for Patrick distracted from his worry about his wife and for those few moments he felt his body relax.

When they arrived at the O'Toole cottage, Maureen's mother had very little to tell them. It was two days the law considered her missing, but five days since she'd last seen her daughter. When Maureen left on a Tuesday morning to meet with Kevin she planned on returning that evening; on Thursday Kevin stopped by, alone, at Maureen's request he said, to check on her and to let her know

Maureen would be gone a couple more days. When Kevin arrived two days later, he was expecting she'd be there or had been there on her way back to Kenora, and was concerned when he learned her mother hadn't seen her. Kevin considered her missing for two days at that point. Then Kevin stopped again the next morning to check for new developments but had none of his own to report. That was the last time she saw him.

"Have you any way of contactin' Kevin?"

"I know he lives in Dublin. I don't have his address; I guess he must have telephone but I don't know his exchange or his number. He owns a music shop, but I'm afraid I don't even know the name of it."

"What is it about Kevin that he seems to be… I don't know, sort of mysteriously orbitin' round your daughter?"

"He had a close friendship with Maureen's da. An' after Donovan died, it was easy for Maureen to let Kevin take on as some sort of a guide."

"He was your husband's good friend, but you can't get in touch with him? If there's anythin' I should know about him that would help me find her—"

Tommy interrupted. "Or find him."

"You've got to tell me right now."

"Maureen told me about your jealously of the man."

"He makes me suspicious, not jealous."

"Just know you're the only man my daughter has ever loved."

"An' I thank you for that, yeah, that is the blessin' of my life, an' so I need to ask you again, if there's anythin' you haven't told me, that might help me know where to look, or what I am lookin' for, you've got to tell me now."

"You don't have to ask me again. I've not slept since Kevin's visit put me in a state, an' I've been thinkin' through all I know or might know or should know for some idea of what's happened. What I have for you I've given; I'm afraid that's it."

The next morning Brian and Tommy called on the local Royal Ulster Constabulary office. The RUC had just discovered her hired car, abandoned near a bridge to the south and east, her night bag on the back seat, and a pistol under the front seat, but no sign of her.

Brian was asked about the pistol.

"It sounds like one of hers. Back home she has a couple of pistols but her .38 is her favorite. She enjoys takin' guests back to the dump, behind our fishin' camp, for target practice. Cans an' bottles. She's got an expert skill at it, at target shootin'."

And when asked he replied, "No, I haven't known her to travel with it."

"It's interesting to note that it appears to have been fired recently. And four times."

"She fired her pistol?"

"We don't know if she fired it or not. When it was found it had just one bullet in the cylinder and it had been fired in the past few days."

Tommy saw a look on his father's face he'd never seen before. He looked frightened.

The look was soon masked.

They got directions to where the car was found and Tommy and Brian drove there. They spent the next two days searching the villages up and down the road and up and down the River, but no one had seen her or heard anything.

Brian and Tommy were sitting in a pub eating cold cuts and cheese at the end of another long day of searching for clues. Brian took a deep drink of the local stout and placed his glass down, slowly, speaking slowly, as he began to accept the thought he'd been fighting.

"She's been missin' for a week, yeah."

"My count is six days."

"Her pistol was shot, four times… She must be…"

He was quiet, he took another drink, Tommy waited, and he then asked, "She must be?"

Brian didn't want to say it. He stared at his glass.

"Isn't it the only conclusion that makes any sense of this? She wouldn't leave us by choice. I know her love for me was real but if I'm wrong it's clear she worships an' adores her Gracie an' would never abandon her willfully. So someone has done somethin' to her, someone stopped her, there at the bridge, where they found her car, as she was headin' to Derry, somehow, for some reason, someone stopped her right there, an' I am beginnin' to think that in the struggle they…"

Brian was quiet. Tommy waited. He was studying his father's face when he saw it change; sadness invaded every feature and Tommy had to look away. They were silent and still. Finally Brian stood and said, "All I've got is feckin' Kevin Coogan. An' if it's not him, he knows who."

❋ ❋ ❋

As they traveled, Brian worked the RUC's chain of command for support for his search. It was on his seventh day in Ireland, when they doubled back to Derry, with Brian growing more and more despondent, that an officer shared important information and the theory the RUC had been considering from the beginning. They had been keeping it from the public, but now they were interested in how Brian would react.

"It's IRA."

Tommy watched for Brian's reaction; he didn't appear surprised.

"What does that mean, it's IRA?"

"You know how turf cutters battle over boundary rights at the edges of their peat fields. There's been a turf war going on between various IRA factions for years, yeah, only now it's getting worse. We heard of skirmishes between them on that very day. We believe she got herself caught in the middle of a turf war."

Brian was silent, so Tommy asked, "What evidence do you have supporting this theory?"

"There were bullet holes in her car. Three of them."

Brian exploded. "Bullet holes! Why the feck wasn't I told about bullet holes in my wife's car!"

Two officers came from another room and stood at the doorway in case they were needed.

"First, sir, you'll control that temper. And you'll understand that we are very careful when and how we share the details of an ongoing investigation."

"Where were they?"

The officer slid a photo of the car from a file and handed it to Brian.

"One in the driver's side window, one in the driver's door, and the front left tire was shot out."

Brian was stunned quiet and his son spoke for him.

"Did you find any blood in the car?"

"No."

"You didn't find any, or you won't tell us?"

"We didn't find any."

Brian found his voice.

"An' how was she involved?"

"We're not saying she was involved. It might be she was simply driving by at the wrong place at the wrong time."

Brian shook his head. "No, no, she's always a right place right time sort of a lady." Then he blurted it out. "You think my wife's IRA."

"Right now we're treating this as an IRA affair, and we suspect she was a casualty."

Though Brian had wondered, he was struck dumb when he heard the officer officially refer to his wife as a casualty. Once again his son spoke for him.

"A casualty? You need a body for a casualty."

"Not always. Missing and presumed dead, that's a casualty."

Brian turned away to try to control himself so Tommy couldn't see his face turning red, early evidence of the Red Bull Demon returning. If he had, he might not have asked his next question.

"Is Kevin Coogan IRA?"

"I heard you were asking after Kevin Coogan. How do you know him?"

Brian's back was still turned but his answer was hot. "He's a friend of my wife's family."

"Yes, we have evidence linking Coogan to a number of known IRA operations."

When Brian turned back to ask his next question, Tommy saw Red Bull Demon's anger.

He wasn't roaring, but he was fuming.

"Any of your evidence point to where the feck he is?"

The police officer didn't respond well to Brian's heat. "One more time, sir, you must calm down. An officer of the Crown won't be spoken to in that tone. We're conducting our investigation, and any further information we have pertinent to the investigation is not information we're sharing with the public at this point."

Tommy winced when the officer said "public." His father didn't. He stepped forward, the Red Bull Demon in charge.

"I hain't the feckin' public. I'm her goddamn husband. So you tell me, do you think Maureen Burke is IRA?"

The RUC officers were all in attendance now.

"You need to leave. We are conducting our investigation and will continue. Any further threating language from you and we will respond with force to restrain you."

Tommy took his father's arm and first Brian resisted but when Tommy whispered "Patrick" he allowed his son to lead him back to their car.

Brian and Tommy were driving south, to Cong, to check on Grace and Mary and talk with Eamon. Once, after they were driving silently for a long distance, Brian spoke in a flat voice "The feckin' IRA." And a few moments later he said, "She never would let me speak ill of the feckin' IRA."

They continued in silence. Tommy stole a glance to see if the Red Bull Demon was gone from his father's face. He appeared more hurt and confused than angry.

They passed Lough Gill, kept heading south as the road turned to Sligo, and they crossed the River.

"The feckin' IRA. She defended them with her full passions an' her sharpest wit."

"Many who do aren't themselves soldiers."

"I never figured hers was anythin' more than some feckin' Irish lost cause patriotism."

"The RUC aren't saying she's one of them. Only she might have gotten in the middle of one of their battles."

With a snort Brian said, "Yeah, what's the chances of that? I mean, if feckin' Kevin Coogan is IRA, then what am I to think about…"

It was evening, and they were all gathered near the peat fire in Eamon's cottage. Mary and Eamon's wife sat at the table; the three men sat closest to the stove. Grace had crawled into her da's lap and soon fell asleep to the low rumble of his voice from deep in his chest.

"Eamon, I need you to be as straight with me as ever you've been, an' tell me if you ever heard anyone wonderin' at all about my Maureen?"

"Wonderin' how so?"

Brian didn't notice he had Mary's attention at the mention of her friend's name.

"About her bein' involved in it, in…" Brian checked on his daughter, saw she was deep asleep, and said softer still, "I… R… A."

Eamon got up to take a pipe off the mantle.

"There was one night, yeah, one night I wondered about it myself."

"Whatta' you say? Why the feck are you just tellin' me now? When?"

Tommy interrupted, "Grace doesn't need to be in the middle of this."

Mary was there before Tommy finished; she picked up the child and cooed in her ear as she carried her to a bed.

Brian had grown angrier waiting for them to leave the room.

"So why the feck are you just tellin' me now?"

"Cause it was just one night I thought it, no more than a night, one night some ol' traveler arrived at the pub an' was tellin' a room full of stories."

"An' what did he say?"

"As I recall it, he started off insistin' Russell had been successful at workin' the Nazis, an' that himself got a chest a' Nazi gold to buy guns."

"That rumor's been floatin' round pubs since the war years. There was a rumor the gold was hid outside of Wicklow that sent a bunch a' fellas on a crazy man's chase searchin' for it, just after the war."

"Well, the story he tells is the fellow that Russell trusted to smuggle this gold into Ireland, well it seems that this fellow an' his girlfriend managed to snag the gold, or most of it, or some of it, as I recall it, he kept changin' that bit, an' then the two smugglers split the bounty an' went their separate ways."

"An' so what's that got to do with Maureen?"

"He said the girlfriend took her share with her to hide somewhere in the great Alaskan wilderness. But then later he said it might have been somewhere in Canada."

"Feckin' hell. You didn't think I should have heard about that?"

"I said to meself I have to let Bri know but this was before we were back in touch you see, when I didn't know where you were. An' anyway, the same fella shows up in the pub a few nights later an' he showed himself to be naught but a crazy one, with all sorts of stories, yeah, with stories that the biggest secret in the world is that the Nazis actually won the war, that they secretly infiltrated the British government at the highest levels you see, an' that Russell learned of this plot, an' that's why they killed him, so, they poisoned him, an' I mean it was all a load a shite, folks was laughin' about it for weeks after."

Tommy asked, "He never spoke Maureen's name?"

"Not him, an' I never heard a word against her name, no."

Eamon handed Brian the pipe he had packed.

"One thing the Brits do right, blendin' tobacco. You'll like this, Number 99."

Brian took the pipe, then stood and walked to the door. Before he opened it, he turned.

"So now I'll be wonderin' was Innish Cove built wit' Nazi money, or worryin's more like it."

Tommy's voice held his father inside. "It's just travelers' tales."

"If what the RUC say is true, then why not this as well? She had nearly four thousand pounds an' not much of a story about where it came from."

"You'd know if it were true. The IRA wouldn't let her get away with their money once they knew she had it."

"They didn't let her get away with it then, did they? Kevin Coogan shows up in Cong when I'm there, then he visits us at Innish Cove unexpectedly. He coulda' been scoutin' for the money, yeah. The whole time we were out fishin' he was askin' questions about the business, an' how much it cost to start it, what we'd invested. Just then the story was we'd just about run out so maybe he was just bidin' his time an' finally they've killed her for it. I've got to find feckin' Coogan an' when I do I'll beat the truth out of him if I have to."

Eamon was finished packing his own pipe. "If it is true, Coz, if your wife had anything to do with IRA, the best thing you can do is go home, right now, take your daughter an' Mary out of this place an' return to your Indians. Have a memorial service for her in that Chapel you an' Tommy built, among them who loved her."

Brian was silent. He opened the door and looked up at the stars, then down the dark road.

Tommy came up behind him.

"You do violence now, you'll never get Patrick back."

Brian looked past his son to his cousin. "You just said I should plan a memorial service."

"I'm sorry if I spoke prematurely."

"I don't think we should give up yet… If anyone has an idea… I need Maureen to tell me what to do next…"

Brian stepped outside in the dark and headed down the path to the road to town to the pub but first called back over his shoulder. "But mark these words. If the IRA ever show up at Innish Cove, they'll find the Red Bull Demon an' his wild Indians waitin'."

He continued walking in the dark and said to himself, "I'll be feckin' lost without her." Then he began to cry.

※ ※ ※

Brian and his mother-in-law stood behind her cottage and waited for Grace with Mary following to wander to the far edge of the yard before Brian told of all he had learned. He had stopped at RUC headquarters before he arrived at the cottage for any further information they had. He hadn't liked what he heard, nor was he surprised by what they told him. They now reported what they called a conviction that Maureen was a casualty in an IRA fight and that she was IRA. When he was finished telling his mother-in-law all he knew, he waited for any information, but none came.

"Can I ask you somethin' about somethin'?"

She answered with silence.

"Their belief is fueled by the fact that your husband himself was an IRA man. So her da, IRA. Her close associate, Kevin Coogan, IRA."

She was still silent.

"They claim more evidence of her affiliation, but that's all they'd share with me... You must have somethin' to say on the subject."

"My Donovan was accused of that many times, for he supported them, he supported them publicly, givin' speeches reproachin' the British an' justifyin' IRA actions. But I don't believe he did anythin' more."

"You don't? 'For directin' terrorist activities against the British Crown' is how they put it to me as the reason he was shot an' killed by the Black n' Tans."

"He was shot an' killed by the Black n' Tans. They got that part right. But it was for the simple reason he spoke the truth."

"An' poor Maureen was forced to watch when they shot him."

"A young girl she was, too, when the murderin' Black n' Tans killed her da, yes."

"An' she never told me. An' you never thought to tell me?"

Maureen's mother had no reply.

"Why'd they shoot him if he wasn't IRA?"

"You need to ask that? Because he was a true Irishman who was never ashamed to say so, loud an' proud. He was a threat to them, for Donovan O'Toole stood in the public square an' named them as evil. Their actions proved him right, wouldn't you say?"

"An' what about any acts of terror that he might have—"

"I don't like this."

"But that's why they think Maureen herself was IRA."

"So they lied about both of 'em and you can't be claimin' that they don't do that all the time. Maureen called it disinformation..."

She turned quickly and walked back to the cottage. Brian spotted Grace in the garden with Mary, then followed his mother-in-law.

"Maureen called what disinformation? When would she be—"

She stopped at the door. "That's enough of this. Stop asking me your questions. Maureen wasn't IRA. My dear husband was not IRA."

Then she slammed the door.

Brian again located his daughter; she was singing to Mary in the garden. He caught Mary's eye, and she nodded that everything was fine. Brian entered the cottage and found his mother-in-law sitting at the table, tears on her face, wringing a cloth in her hands. She looked up at him and spoke in a near whisper.

"I'm arranging a memorial service for my daughter. In two days."

"A memorial service. That means you've given up hope she lives."

She didn't answer. He sat across from her.

"So you're sayin' I need to go out to the garden an' tell Grace O'Malley her mum is never comin' back. She's not missin'. She's dead."

She didn't respond.

"Look..."

"No, you look. I know my daughter. She'd be here if she could. If she can't, that can only mean one thing."

"That someone killed her. That she's dead."

"You said yourself that the RUC are treating her as a casualty."

"Sure, but..."

"I just know... I... just know."

And finally, for the first time, Brian did too.

❊ ❊ ❊

Brian sat at the table, trying to find a way to tell his daughter this terrible news. He found her with Mary in the garden. He asked Mary to stay with them then sat down next to his daughter on the garden bench. Mary stood right behind them.

"I want to see Mum."

Brian wrapped his arms around her and hugged her close.

"Will you try somethin' for your da, my Gracie girl?"

"I want to see Mum."

"An' I want you to, an' so I'm askin' you to try somethin' now for Da. It's a new game we're gonna learn to play together."

"Will I see Mum?"

"If you do what I say now, I hope so."

"What do I do?"

"You start by closin' your eyes, an' get cozy comfy. Give me just a little smile, to show me you're ready to play this game with Da… Ah, such a lovely smile you've got an' how many times have I said your smile is the perfect picture of Mum's smile…"

Mary closed her eyes too, and a trace of a smile graced her face as she followed Brian's prompts to see her dear friend.

"Keep your eyes closed now, an' listen to my voice. I want you to pretend I am tellin' you a story. I want you to find that place you go…" Brian gently patted her head. "…when you want to see pictures of the stories Mum tells you when you're lyin' in your bed at night—"

Eyes closed, Grace interrupted. "When Mum tells me stories about when Grace O'Malley is a pirate I can see her sailing ships."

"Well just like you see those pictures of sailin' ships, just like you see those pictures, I want you to make a picture of my Gracie girl, of you an' of Little Stevie, together, playin' under your table, in the kitchen at the Lodge. You're playin' with the animal carvin' Old George gave ya, you've got Otter, yeah, an' he's jumpin' over your favorite stones, an' Little Stevie is playin' with ya…"

"He has the piece of wood where Nigig likes to dance."

"That's right, an' while you an' Little Stevie are playin' together you can hear all the women workin' around you, an' the pots a' clangin' an' water is runnin' an' Little Stevie is laughin' an' laughin' an' then he's tellin' you that he'll always be there next to you, an' then you can hear Mum callin' you…"

"She says, 'Now Mary, where is my Gracie Girl?' "

"Yes, that's right, that's just how she says it, she's sayin' your name like she loves to say it, an' then there she is, peekin' under the table, lookin' down at you an' smilin'. You can see her. She's so beautiful an' she loves you so much."

"I see her."

Mary nodded her head. She saw her, too. She whispered a prayer for her dear friend.

"Tell me what she's wearin'?"

"She's wearing her red blouse… Where are you Mum? Da and I miss you."

"Now Gracie, I want you to tell Mum that Da needs you. So

tell her you'll be back later, an' open your eyes… you saw her clear, yeah?"

"I saw her."

"Well honey, I need to tell you that I've been lookin' an' lookin' for days an' days for Mum. I've searched the mountaintops, an' I searched the valleys an' I couldn't find her. I've searched the towns an' the villages, an' I can't find her there neither."

Grace leaned away from her father so she could look at his face.

"Have you searched the bogs?"

"Yes, we've searched the bogs."

"In Mum's stories the little baby lamb got lost in the bogs."

"I've searched the bogs; I've searched everywhere an' I can't find her anywhere."

"Where did she go?"

"Well, Gracie girl, I have found some men who think they know where she's gone. They think she's gone to Heaven."

Grace pulled away and sat straight up.

"That means they think she's not alive anymore?"

"Yes Gracie girl, I am afraid that's what it means. It means they think she's died, an' gone to Heaven where she's smilin' down on you an' livin' forever more in your stories."

Grace O'Malley started to cry. Mary started to cry.

"What did you say to those men when they said that?"

Tears gathered in Brian's eyes. He couldn't speak.

"Did you tell them they're wrong?"

"No, I didn't."

"Why didn't you?"

Grace sobbed softly.

"What men told you that?"

Brian was crying. Mary was crying.

"They are policemen, like our Mounties."

She was sobbing deeply, and looked at Mary.

"Little Stevie does not like the Mounties."

"Yes, well, only some Mounties are mean to the Indians. Not all the Mounties are bad."

She cried in his arms; he cried as he held her; Mary leaned forward to touch them both.

"I know Mum loves her Grace O'Malley so much that before she went to Heaven she left a big part of her livin' inside you. She's livin' inside your dreams, an' she's livin' inside your heart. She lives in the stories we will tell each other about her, an' she lives in your love, Gracie girl, in the love that you an' I share, that Mary an' Little Stevie and Joe Loon all share… An' she lives forever at Innish Cove. She loves you so much she'll be waitin' for you any time you need to tell her somethin'."

They sat together, Mary stood over them, and Grace slowly stopped crying. When she spoke, still tight in her father's arm, Brian heard the sounds of Maureen's voice.

"Mum said when she went to heaven that she would make shore lunch for the angels."

"She… when did she tell you that?"

"We were in my bedroom. It was part of a story she told me when she was teaching me how to pack my suitcase. She took a trip up to heaven and her job was to make shore lunch for all the angels."

Brian looked to Mary for evidence of her understanding but she hadn't heard this before.

"Do you remember more of the story?"

She started crying again. "Oh Mum. I miss you Mum." Her crying grew.

Mary placed her hand on the girls shoulder. "She will always love you."

"I will always love her."

Maureen's memorial service was to be held at Saint Columba's, in the Long Tower Chapel, in the center of Derry, where Maureen's parents had each been baptized and were married, where all of their children were baptized, and where Donovan O'Toole's funeral mass had been conducted with pews overflowing and plenty of RUC quietly watching.

Maureen's service would begin shortly. Brian and Tommy met with the presiding priest in a sitting room, in the undercroft. The priest asked if Tommy intended to vest; Tommy wanted to sit with his family but was able to convince the priest to bend liturgical rules so he could say a few words about Maureen before the concluding rites.

After the priest left the cramped room, Katie led Grace and Mary in, and they sat together waiting for the service to start. Katie sang a Celtic hymn in a soft voice to her little sister, and Tommy, Grace, and Mary were comforted though Brian took little notice.

"...Take the wave now and know you are free. Your back's to the land, as you turn to the sea. Face the wind now, so wild and so strong. When you think of me, wave to me, and sing me your song..."

It was near time to start the service when Eamon came in to announce, "He's here."

Tommy was frightened by the look in his father's eye when Brian said, "Kevin Coogan?" It was the rage of his demon that had been surfacing more and more over the past days, a rage that caused Tommy to decide he would stick close to his father's side until he was boarding his plane home.

"It's Patrick. I left him standin' in the narthex."

"Patrick came? Will he sit with us?"

Tommy said, "I hadn't expected he'd come at all. Let him find his place."

Brian sat in the first pew, between his two daughters; Tommy sat next to Katie, Maureen's mother sat next to Grace, and Maureen's two older sisters sat next to their mother; they left an empty space between them in honor of Donovan O'Toole. Eamon and his wife were in the pew behind them, with Mary; other family members filled it and the next pews were crowded with Derry folk and many who traveled from Cong.

Patrick had waited for his family to process past him—he greeted his brother and sisters; Brian smiled but Patrick looked away—and then at a distance he followed them in, choosing to sit not with the family but two rows behind the last of the crowded pews.

Soon after the service began, Kevin arrived outside the church with two men from his brigade; they had traveled to Derry separately and still kept a distance from each other. The two men entered the church first, one at a time, and when they didn't return it indicated to Kevin all was safe for him to enter. He waited a few minutes more and then went in.

Tommy rose to deliver his remarks and when he looked out over the pews to find Patrick he saw Kevin Coogan was seated right behind him. Tommy recognized him—Kevin had been toasted for two days as the hero of Cong after he saved the young girl from the runaway carriage—and when Brian saw his son's face change he turned to see what was wrong. The heads and shoulders of family and friends in the pews behind Brian blocked much of his view, so he turned back as Tommy began to speak.

"The most satisfying truth I have found in my devotion to Him is that His plans will always be shrouded in mystery. For his mystery is beauty. His mystery is in the beauty of a flower. Why should a structure of such practical purpose bring delight to those of us who have no role in the flower's continued existence? I can never understand why that is, but it appears that it must be so, as each and every flower has its own blossoming beauty, and so I find wisdom in the acceptance of the mystery of His gifts…"

Brian was listening to his son, but he was also curious what had brought that look of concern to his face, a concern that still marked him. Brian was afraid it meant Patrick had left, that Tommy had looked for him in the pews and not seen him.

As Tommy continued, Kevin found himself on his knees, praying for Maureen. He had loved her, first like a daughter, then as a sister and fellow freedom fighter, so he prayed for her eternal rest and he prayed for forgiveness, and he prayed for justice.

Kevin didn't know the young man he could reach out and touch just in front of him was Brian's son; Patrick had been a boy of ten when they met before and was nearly eighteen now. Kevin had chosen this spot so he could see the whole crowd in front of him, for while he was mourning Maureen, he was wary.

Tommy paused when he saw Kevin kneel to pray, then continued.

"…a greater mystery then is man. Our practical purpose for our lives in this world is to complete His Creation, and we ourselves are created as a divinely wrought beauty, yet how often it seems that each of them, our sense of purpose and our exquisite beauty, is corrupted by the other…"

Brian decided Patrick was still there. If he were to leave early he'd at least wait until Tommy finished.

Before he knelt to pray, Kevin had spotted his two men, one to his left, one to his right, both blending in by sitting right at the edges of the crowded pews.

"…I have seen the work Maureen O'Toole Burke took up, with such care, such devotion, on a lovely wilderness River where God's children live, where every day she prayed 'God bless the Innocents,' where she fought to protect a profound expression of the Great Creator's beauty from the corruption of man's avarice and arrogance…"

Kevin stumbled in his prayer when the words 'God bless the Innocents' broke through.

Patrick leaned away from the man who had sat right behind him and prayed at his shoulder so close that he added to Patrick's anxiety, so close he could hear the stranger whisper Maureen's name and could feel the sadness that shrouded him.

When Tommy was finished and returned to the family, Brian leaned to him to whisper, "Is Patrick still there?" Tommy looked concerned but nodded yes. Then Brain leaned over again and said, "God bless the Innocents. Sure."

And Tommy nodded, then shook his head.

The service ended and the Burke and O'Toole families prepared to rise from the pews as the priest approached, his Latin chant filling the church. As they stood, Brian felt Tommy's hand on his arm and turned to see that the look of concern on his son's face had deepened.

He held his father there so Katie could slip by them.

"Let her pass. I need you to listen to me."

"I won't approach him."

"What?"

"Tell Patrick I'll leave him be."

The family had begun shuffling out of the pews, collecting

and organizing themselves in the aisles; when Mary saw Brian was talking with his son she took Grace O'Malley by the hand. The chanting priest paused for them to form behind him, but Tommy held Brian where they stood, their backs to those in the pews, then he hugged his father, one Brian was eager to return, for it was the first time he'd been hugged by any of his children since the day he had beaten baby Patrick.

The priest began his recession, unaware he wasn't immediately followed; the family waited for Brian and Tommy.

Brian was crying.

"I don't care what she's done, I can't live—"

"Listen to me Brian. Don't let go, and listen to what I have to say." Tommy's hug became a tight hold. "Seated just behind Patrick, there's a man on his knees praying for the soul of Maureen Burke." Brian started to turn. "No, no, don't look, you won't see but the top of his head, but I must prepare you, for it's Kevin Coogan."

Brian's strength dwarfed his son's and he easily broke out of Tommy's arms to look out over the folks in the pews, many of whom were beginning to wonder about the priest walking alone and this show of what had first appeared to be a son's loving comfort of his father's deep despair but was suddenly taking on a harder tone; those who knew Brian grew fearful of the fierce red edge replacing the tears on his face.

First Brian saw Patrick but took no notice of the quick flash of fear on Patrick's face, for Brian was searching for Kevin and there he was, behind his son, his head bent in prayer.

Tommy had used the moment to step past Brian to stand before his exit from the pew.

"Listen to me Brian."

They both spoke softly so only they heard each other.

"Maureen's killer has the feckin' nerve—"

"We don't know he's the killer."

Tommy turned to lead his father out of the pew to the waiting family.

"What the feck would he be prayin' for?"

"You have to control yourself."

Someone had gotten the priest's attention and he stopped and waited, though he continued his song cycle.

Brian didn't take his eyes off of Kevin.

Patrick had to look away from his father's stare, and his stomach was growing sour; his head was light. He leaned forward and put his head in his hands while the family formed itself in the aisle, waiting for Tommy and Brian.

Tommy spoke to the whole family, and especially Eamon.

"Brian will recess with all of you, and Eamon come take my place next to your cousin. I am going to go talk with Kevin Coogan." Brian's stare never wavered; his face was red. "I will arrange for a time and a place for them to have the conversation they need to have. But we're in a church Brian, and I want you to promise all of us here—"

"I know exactly where we are."

The family turned to walk down the aisle to join the priest, and Eamon took his place on Brian's left, so he'd be between Brian and Kevin as they passed his pew.

As they walked Brian never looked away from the man he saw as his wife's killer, and neither Kevin in his prayer nor Patrick in his fear looked up, but Kevin's men had noticed the interest Brian and Tommy and Eamon were taking in Kevin, and each of them slowly slid down their pews to sit at the aisle, ready to move.

Tommy took his eyes off Brian just long enough to quickly turn to the altar and bow and then he turned back. His plan was to wait until the family had passed the first filled pews, follow them, then slip in next to Kevin and arrange for Brian to talk with him as soon as Brian was calm.

The family joined the priest at the edge of the crowded pews and continued on, at the priest's solemn pace. Katie had taken Grace's hand from Mary and they walked just in front of their father and Uncle Eamon; Mary, enchanted by it all, followed behind. As they drew near, Patrick sensed it and looked up and Katie saw by the empty sadness of his face that her brother shouldn't have come. She smiled at him, but he didn't return it.

At the same time the family drew even with these pews, Kevin looked up from his prayer and sat back. When his eyes met Brian's for the first time Brian stopped while everyone ahead moved on.

Tommy walked quickly to join them; Kevin's men were alert, and Patrick began to shake.

Brian snarled, "I've been lookin' for you."

Kevin was quiet. Patrick shook harder. The priest didn't falter. Katie turned at her father's voice, as did the rest of the family, and she separated herself from the family to slide into the pew next to her brother. She pulled his head onto her shoulder. "He's talking to the man behind you."

Eamon urged his cousin on. "We're goin' to talk to him later Brian; you're promised a private meetin'."

Brian stood there, in the aisle, looking past Patrick and Katie at Kevin.

"The RUC says you IRA killed her."

Kevin pursed his lips.

Tommy took his father's arm. "We act to honor Maureen."

Brian was surprised by his own response. "Maybe she *loved* the violence. Maybe that's *why* she married me."

Kevin's men joined the family, waiting to see what came next. Kevin shook his head, indicating they should stand down, then rose to leave from the other end of the pew. Brian's anger erupted, and he roared "Don't turn your feckin' back on what you did!" as he yanked his arm from his son and pushed his cousin aside who stumbled out of the way when he tripped over the end of the pew.

Brian tried to move quickly down the pew after Kevin and the awkward struggle of the narrow passage simply angered him more. Patrick looked up with terror in his eyes to see his father rushing towards him, then towering over him as he passed, then turned to see him throw himself into the man who had reached the end of the pew, and they landed together with a thud on the church's stone floor.

Brian pinned Kevin under him; Kevin spoke for Brian's ear only. "The Brits killed her Brian. It was the Brits who killed her," and he struggled to reach for the pistol in his coat pocket. Brian wrestled for the opening to throw a punch and that allowed Kevin to secure the pistol and when he had a good grip he pressed it to Brian's belly, hidden from the view of the others, including Tommy and Eamon, and Kevin's two men who had been navigating the pews to join them, and the rest who stood to watch or got up from the prayers to leave, some running.

Patrick had pulled away from his sister and slid down the pew away from the battle, feeling more and more faint, the slow growth of a spell beginning to accelerate, then rush. He was determined to leave the source of it, but when Patrick stood, the great surge of the spell swallowed him whole and he blacked out and collapsed; as he was going down he hit his head hard with a loud bang on the edge of the pew. Katie saw it, and heard it, and felt it. "Patrick!" She was at his side in an instant.

When Brain felt the pistol barrel press into him, he froze.

"You're too smart to use that on me here."

"If you leave me no choice. But I warn you, Brian. While there's many who sympathize with your grief, they will still accept it as their duty to do you one notch worse than whatever you do to me."

The four men had formed a semi-circle around them, and were at the ready.

"I was her friend, Brian. Count me among those who loved her."

"Then you should have protected her."

"I told her to leave."

"Tell me why she came."

"There are questions I won't answer." He pressed the pistol deeper into Brian's stomach. "Now get off of me."

Brian climbed off of Kevin and they both stood, though Brian held tight to Kevin's coat.

Maureen's sisters joined Katie at Patrick's side; he lay in the aisle, unconscious. Mary collected Grace and led her away from danger.

Kevin held his pistol at the ready in his coat pocket. Brian gripped him so close the two men would be nose to nose if Brian weren't inches taller.

"I came to show my respects."

"What the feck does that mean comin' from you?"

"And I came to tell you I am sorry for your loss, but I know for certain it was the British who killed her."

Brian's fist tightened its clench on Kevin's coat, and Kevin felt the need to raise his pistol again.

"You know that for certain."

"That's right, with rogue RUC pulling the trigger on the gun."

Tommy stepped forward. "Let's continue this conversation in private."

Brian ignored him and asked Kevin, "Why?"

"That's another question I won't answer."

"If RUC killed her, she must be IRA." They stood facing each other, staring, and then Kevin slowly removed his hand from his pocket.

"I let go of the gun. Now you let go of me."

Brian didn't loosen his grip.

"My advice is you and Grace O'Malley return to your Eden and leave our troubles behind."

"An Eden built with IRA money?"

Kevin hesitated just long enough for Brian to guess he was right, then said, "I can promise you, Brian, you've no worries there."

"I don't have to worry that I've infected life on the River with the sins of you murdering innocents…" He pushed Kevin away hard.

The priest stood over the women attending to Patrick. Katie had removed her sweater and made a pillow for his head, but except for his breathing he showed no sign of life. She called out to her father and brother and uncle. "Patrick's hurt bad. He bashed his head on the pew as he was falling from a faint."

Tommy and Eamon turned at her voice; Brian hesitated just a moment.

"I don't want to see you or hear from you ever again. So tell me all I need to know to get on with my life."

"You know Maureen was a wonderful woman, and you're safe in your camp with your daughter and your Indians." Then Kevin walked away, and his men stood on guard until they were certain Brian was returning to his family.

When a damp cloth across his brow failed to revive Patrick, the priest sent an altar boy to fetch the local doctor. Someone found a pillow to replace Katie's sweater under Patrick's head, then a cushion for Katie to sit on, for she wouldn't leave her brother's side. She held his hand and caressed his face, and slowly rocked back and forth.

When first Brian joined the family and saw his son out cold on the floor, his confusion about what happened was soon replaced with the understanding that it was somehow the result of his own actions. The look from Katie as he knelt next to her confirmed it, and the condemning tone in her voice as she explained what happened drove him away. Tommy led him to a pew where he sat, his head in his hands, Tommy at his side.

Another minute passed when Katie felt her brother's hand jerk and he came awake. "Don't get up. Stay there. We've a doctor coming to look at you. You fainted and hit your head on the pew."

Patrick raised his hand and held it over the side of his head, just above the temple, where he'd received the blow, where the pain was dull but deep, then rubbed his eye with the heel of that hand.

"How long was I out?"

"Maybe four or five minutes."

Patrick lay on his back, looking up at his sister, collecting his thoughts and memories of what had happened.

"A double."

"What?"

"A double."

"What's a double?"

"I fainted and then I was knocked out."

"Yes, I guess that's right."

"Is he still here?"

"He wasn't coming after you; it was some fellow messed up in Maureen's death who was sitting right behind you."

"I know. I saw him tackle the man and knock him to the ground…Make him leave."

"Tommy is talking to him about—"

"Make him leave right now. But first you tell him this was his last chance."

"Let me get Tommy for you."

❄ ❄ ❄

When Tommy left to speak with Patrick, Mary led Grace to her father, and she sat next to him. Mary stepped back but stayed attentive. Brian was still crouched over in the pew, his head in his hands. Grace put her hand on his knee.

"I love your mother so much Gracie Girl, that I hurt deep inside."

"Me too."

Brian looked up, then put his arm around her and held her close.

"That was the bad man who made Mum go away to heaven?"

"Yes."

"Then I'm glad you hurt him."

Tommy returned, saw Grace, and asked Mary to distract her one more time.

"God damn your anger."

"Is he goin' to be all right?"

"He's never going to be all right; you don't seem to understand that."

"I mean this knock to his head."

"The doctor's just arrived to examine him. But Patrick wants you to leave right now."

"Just as soon as I know he's going to be—"

"He wants you to leave now, and he doesn't want to see you ever again. Brian, your son Patrick asked me to tell you to stay away from him from now on."

"He just said that now?"

"He said this was your last chance."

Brian motioned to Mary to bring Grace to him.

"We'll drive to Dublin now an' fly home on the first plane we can get on."

"I'll send word about what the doctor says about this head injury."

"An' you'll pray for me."

"Without ceasing."

On the plane ride home Brian told the stewardess to bring him two whiskeys. When the plane landed in LaGuardia there were six small empty bottles in the seat pocket before him, and he had three more tucked in his coat pocket for the flight to Winnipeg.

The first whiskeys soothed Brian's pain; the next whiskeys fueled his anger. He loved and adored her, and she deceived him, perhaps betrayed him. When he looked at their daughter sleeping in the seat next to him, he became angrier still, and drank another.

By the time they landed in Winnipeg Brian was drunk and dazed from believing that Maureen was IRA, that the money used to build the camp was IRA money, and that it was a stain on all they had built together, the two of them, with Joe Loon and his clan, and Dutch.

In the wake of his first wife Deidre's death, when his pain was not just the sadness of the world spoiled, when it was compounded by profound shame and guilt, he found comfort in the bottle. He looked for it there again, first thing and all day.

The comfort he found in a bottle a day led Brian to decide he wouldn't open the Great Lodge at Innish Cove the next season. He intended to ask Dutch to contact all of the guests who had booked reservations and let them know about Maureen passing and to share with them Brian's sincere apologies that the Great Lodge at Innish Cove wouldn't open again until the following season, Spring of 1960.

But those intentions didn't last long. When he met with his accountant and attorney they walked him through the business' finances and their tally of the obligations he would have regardless—a substantial land lease payment, for starters. He understood he had no choice, and that he needed the cash flow or risked losing everything. He would open. He had to.

That meant he had to cut back on his drinking; he couldn't maintain this pace in camp. He moderated, a bit, some of the time; he told himself he would cut back even more when he needed to, when the opening of the new season approached, now that he had his drinking under control.

And when Grace was in bed, when she was deep in sleep, he would finish the bottle he started earlier as he took up cursing Maureen O'Toole all night long until he cried his sorrows for Maureen Burke, his Lady Girl, and finally passed into a fitful sleep, dreaming of dangers lurking in shadows.

Dutch saw what was happening to Brian and tried to find ways to care for him. He figured out how every incoming guest could be notified about Maureen's passing. Since each guest had to check in at the NOA offices in Kenora before they boarded their bush plane to Innish Cove, he told Brian it would be handled there, that before each guest boarded a bush plane they would be told Maureen died, in peaceful circumstances, during a visit to Ireland.

When Brian realized he wouldn't have to continually explain to everyone all summer long what happened to his wife, and that he wouldn't have to deal with their shock and their natural curiosity and their demanding questions about the circumstances, he was able to moderate his drinking even more, much of the time.

Chapter 10

HEMINGWAY'S TROPHY

IT PROMISED TO BE AN EXTRAORDINARY EVENT, and Brian's anticipation was growing. Ernest Hemingway had arrived on the last bush plane in to the Great Lodge at Innish Cove the day before, accompanied by three friends. Their arrival was expected, but they had surprised Brian when they unloaded a large wooden crate and promised a great unveiling, in the dining hall after supper the next day, and all in honor of dear Maureen's passing. They told Brian that all he had to do was introduce them in the morning to the best handyman in camp and then stay out of the dining hall until supper.

The first evening the Hemingway foursome was in camp Brian joined them in the pub and was surprised to find how strong his memories were of his wife caring for this man, how she had pampered him and how she anticipated his needs, so subtle, so graceful. And throughout she had let him know she respected his vigor. Brian was pleased to remember her calling him Papa as she held his arm, and when Brian went to bed that night it was with rich, full dreams of his Lady Girl.

His anticipation of the big event that night with Papa Hemingway and with his guests in attendance called upon Brian to take an extra drink or two during the afternoon to be ready, to play Big Irish, the exaggerated version of himself he knew the writer and his guests would enjoy. Brian found he was playing Big Irish more often; it was helping him make it through this first season without Maureen Burke at his side and with Maureen O'Toole's secrets haunting him.

Hemingway's boat was usually one of the first back, and Brian timed his drinking so he was filled with the spirits that brought a full smile and deep laughter to the tired old man. Brian met his boat at the dock, and they stood together telling stories while the bustle of guests and guides swirled about them, pleased to be in their presence, listening when they could.

When the Hemingway party left the dock to head to the Great Lodge to check on preparations for the evening, Brian watched the writer's slow and uneven gait and remembered again how his wife had been so quick to help the old man feel less like an old man, and he was eager to spend more time with his Lady Girl during the unveiling that night, then again in his dreams.

❀ ❀ ❀

The last of the boats were in. Guests were in their cabins showering and napping, and drinking. The guides were putting away supplies and cleaning their boats. With the upcoming celebration of his Lady Girl on his mind, Brian headed to his house. He walked up the path through the trees, sharing hellos with guests sitting on their cabin porches and stopped in the Great Lodge kitchen, showing himself in case he was needed. He wasn't, so he picked up the path behind the Great Lodge that led past the Chapel up the rise to his house.

As he approached the Chapel he was surprised by a strong impulse to stop and go in, and to sit at the statue his wife loved.

He had been avoiding the statue since the camp opened. It was where his wife asked God to bless the innocents. He had heard it as the sweet devotion of his Lady Girl when she said it. Now he knew it as Maureen O'Toole's confession and penitence.

The pull was strong to stop, but he was eager to see his daughter—he saw so much of his Lady Girl in their child—so he resisted and headed up the private path to his house.

❀ ❀ ❀

This was the first summer, the summer she'd turn six, that Grace

O'Malley had the run of the camp. She had already gotten into and out of every kind of trouble and was quick to learn what she should from each close call. Little Stevie, seven, was always by her side, guiding her away from some of her most daring inclinations and often part of her rescue team. Mary had a mother's watchful eye for both of them, and all those who lived or worked there knew it was their job to help take care of the two children.

New daily patterns were emerging that season, adapting to the absence of Maureen's presence.

In the late afternoon when the boats started coming in from the day spent fishing the River and its lakes, Mary would find the children and keep them with her. Then she stopped at the Lodge kitchen to provide extra help during peak supper prep or when the camp was filled with guests; the children still enjoyed playing together under the table, and Grace loved it especially; it often felt as if she was spending time with her mum then and there.

Grace heard her mum's voice in the sounds of the busy kitchen.

After Mary's kitchen help was no longer needed, she would serve their portion of supper and take it up to the house where she and Brian and Grace and Little Stevie shared their meal in the small dining room.

After supper, Brian spent an hour with his daughter, alone in her bedroom while she got ready for bed, asking about her day and listening to her stories, singing songs together, and laughing and talking about Gracie's mother when Grace chose to, and she always did, before he headed down to the Great Lodge to host his guests.

Because the Great Lodge's pub and billiards lounge were filled every night with guests needing Brian's attention, Mary and Little Stevie had moved in to Brian's home so she could help look after Grace; it was a temporary fix that had lasted the first full month the camp had been open, and it was working well for Brian.

Once he left Grace behind in Mary's care his Big Irish character came out to play, to fuel the guests' enthusiasms and enjoy them for himself. To forget everything but the fun of stories told well and men's free laughter.

Mary enjoyed taking care of Grace, and she loved her mastery of the new work Brian was asking her to do, helping him manage the camp. She missed her family and friends at Joe Loon's village, but living out of the spare bedroom with her son was working fine for her as well.

She told Joe Loon, and later she told Brian, that she took it all on as an act of devotion for her departed sister.

❄ ❄ ❄

Upon entering the Great Lodge Brian looked for and found the evidence of what he suspected had been transported in the shipping crate; high on the dining hall wall a large sheet covered what he figured was one of Hemingway's African safari trophy heads. A regular and favorite guest's black bear head that had been moved to make room at the most prominent spot for this new mount, at the head of the dining hall. The crate had been large and long, and the cloth that hid the head hung six feet or more.

Guests finished eating then collected in the pub and the billiards lounge. The guests who had eaten in the first supper seating were returning from their cabins. Hemingway reclaimed his corner, near the fireplace, and was there with old friends and new. The tables were being cleared and the floor was swept.

Drinks were flowing; the laughter was building.

Brian was behind the bar checking inventories of beer in the cooler. When a guest walked up Brian, stood and summoned his grand Irish brogue greeting and offered to pour him any one of the Irish whiskies he chose. "Ya' can't be wrong, each carries twilight's magic, yeah. An' on such an auspicious occasion as this, it's on the house." He sent the guest back to the growing celebratory energy of the room with a smile, promising to join them in a moment. Brian knelt again, checking the cooler, and the guest stopped short, looked over the bar at Brian's big back, and asked, "So then, where is Maureen hiding out?"

Brian stood straight up in surprise and smashed the top of his head on the edge of the shelf that held the row of Irish whiskey bottles. He staggered and nearly fell from the blow that sent an electric shock down his neck, and the question itself knocked him off balance and he gripped the bar to right himself. He hurt most from holding in the roar of angry pain.

"Ow. Brian, that must have hurt… you okay?"

When Brian heard the man's genuine concern, and though he was still woozy from hitting his head, he realized he mistook the question. This wasn't someone sneaking up behind him, someone emerging from Maureen O'Toole's shadow life to torment him, letting Brian know that he knew she'd never been found. No, he realized late, this must be the first guest who somehow got through Dutch's notification system. This guest was simply wondering where Maureen was, and why she wasn't there for this unveiling in her honor.

So Brian explained that Maureen had passed. Watching the raw emotion take control of this man's face, his sadness and his embarrassment, Brian struggled to maintain his own composure as he tried to sooth the guest's pain, for Brian was beginning to feel raw himself.

"I'm so sorry."

It helped to stay in character, the Big Irish.

"We all are. T'was not another like that woman in all the world."

"I don't know what else to say; I'm so sorry."

"Yes, well, we wouldn't be here now, would we, no, no, none of us, any of us, none of this, if it weren't for that... for her, yeah, an' what she did, to make this... look, I regret that you found out so, like this, right now, but if I cause ya' no offense an' if ya' don't mind, I don't really..." and Brian had to leave right then; he felt the Red Bull Demon overtaking Big Irish, so he retreated through the swinging doors to the kitchen, leaving a concerned guest behind.

Brian kept going, through the kitchen out into the night and he found the darkest corner behind the Great Lodge where he tried to hide from what was rising fast and coming on strong out of his misinterpreting the guest's innocent question: all the questions that attach to the memory of Maureen O'Toole, his wife as IRA soldier fighting... fighting how? Not in battles but in ambush? Secretly hiding bombs? Kidnapping? How many? When? She had remarked about the coincidence that she had been in Ireland visiting her mother at the time of the massive arms raid on the Ebrington Barracks arsenal; he heard it as her teasing him then, and recently decided, knowing her brilliance, that she must have been a part of it, perhaps a leader of it, perhaps the leader of it. These questions with no answers made him angrier at her and even angrier at himself.

Now the Red Bull Demon was in full control.

He drank deeply from his flask and returned it to his boot. In a deep low growl he said "God Bless the Innocents," and he spit out a bad taste in his mouth. Then he turned to face the log wall he had been leaning against. He retrieved his flask and took one more deep drink, draining it. With the flask back in his boot he assumed a fighter's posture. "I wonder how many innocents died to build this feckin' place." His head hurt and he wanted to obliterate the pain so he quickly stepped forward into the head butt he delivered against the wall with all his might, with full purpose, and he hit so hard he knocked himself out, crumpling to the ground where he lay, in the darkness, unconscious.

❈ ❈ ❈

Inside the Great Lodge guests were drinking and laughing and smoking pipes and big cigars while admiring the sweeping array of ten point buck heads and twenty five pound northern pike mounted in fighting poses, and all the other trophies and framed photographs. Someone had started a pool for guests to guess what was hidden under the sheet. It was easy to figure it was a sharp horned antelope; some guests guessed it was an eland, others a sable, and others a gemsbok. The guest who just learned of Maureen's death found his friends and tried to figure out how he didn't know what everyone else knew. Papa Hemingway was collecting himself to lead the ceremony and looked around for Brian, and when he didn't see the big man he asked a friend to find him to let him know he was ready to begin.

Just then, and for no apparent reason—perhaps one too many curious guests lifted it for a peek—the sheet that covered the animal head slipped, and slipped, and then floated to the floor, revealing Hemingway's trophy. The guests cheered when they saw it.

❈ ❈ ❈

Mary sat up with a start. She had fallen asleep in a chair in the living room after putting Little Stevie and Grace to bed. There was a reason she woke suddenly, she knew it, and she quickly checked on the children. They slept curled in two little balls, side by side, peacefully. She often allowed them to sleep together in her bed, and she was fine sleeping on the pallet of blankets and pillows on the floor set up for Little Stevie.

Before she went back to sleep Mary had to find what awakened her. She returned to the chair to recapture the feel of it. Perhaps there was something going on at Joe Loon's village? No, it was closer than that, much closer. She returned to her bedroom and awakened Little Stevie, picked him up, and carried him to the living room. "You need to be awake. I must go to the lodge kitchen and check on something for the morning. You stay awake here until I get back."

In a small and sleepy voice Little Stevie said, "Yes, *nimaamaa*."

"You are awake now son. You must care for your sister Grace."

More alert, Little Stevie repeated in a more serious voice, "Yes, *nimaamaa*."

She slipped on her boots and headed out to follow the path through the dark forest, looking, listening, searching for an understanding of what had awakened her so.

As Mary headed down the slope, This Man emerged from the sacred birch grove just behind the Chapel. With him was the spirit of the great warrior of the River, Mathew Loon. They were joined by many of the spirits of those who burned on the funeral pyres that once covered this shoreline with ash. Together they sang for a new spirit that was also an old spirit.

They had been waiting for this new visitor who was also an old visitor for some time now.

Mary sensed their presence as she drew near; she was led to the door of the Chapel, and believing she was awakened for this, she entered. When she did, she felt welcomed. Mary was drawn to the bench that sat in front of the statue of Joseph and his son Jesus. She sat there, as her sister Maureen had done, day after day.

This Man and the warrior spirit of Mathew Loon and the spirits of the Ojibway who died from the white man's pox waited at the sacred birch grove, the trees watered by the tears of those who watched their family members and clan members burn while waiting for their own time.

As Brian became aware he struggled to sit up. He didn't know how or why he was on the ground in the middle of the night. He shook his head to clear the fog but stopped from the pain of it. He thought he was supposed to be inside this log building, but he couldn't recall why. With one hand on the log wall for support he tried to stand, but he couldn't, not yet. He was shaky, his head hurt, his neck hurt. He touched his head, just above the hairline, at the source of the new pain; his fingers were sticky and bloodstained when he pulled them away.

He tried again to stand, fought off the nausea, but then a wave of dizziness brought him to his knees. When it passed he rose again and slowly made his way towards the kitchen door. He thought about the Chapel—he remembered its call to him earlier, and there it was again—but the Chapel was all the way across the clearing and seemed even farther than that now. It seemed a world away, and he was sure he was needed inside, so again he ignored its pull.

The kitchen door flew open and the guest who had asked about Maureen stepped out. The sight of him immediately infuriated Brian, though he wasn't sure why.

"We've been looking for you Brian, Mr. Hemingway wants to… hey, you okay?"

The mention of the writer's name and Brian's anger with this man standing in front of him helped Brian begin to remember, that Hemingway had arrived in camp the day before with… a wooden crate… a big wooden create, a big and long wooden crate, and there was something dead inside it… covered in a burial shroud? In his confused state he wondered if it was Maureen O'Toole's body in the crate, that the IRA soldier had been found and delivered to him, and the shock that came and went with this idea helped him clear his thinking some more. Now he remembered. He brushed past the guest as if he were a nuisance.

❊ ❊ ❊

Hemingway's trophy was a world-class gemsbok, a female. Her horse-shaped head was intelligently beautiful, her horns stellar. All together she was magnificent.

The face was black with what looked like white butterfly shaped sunglasses, oversized, perched across her brow, just above her eyes, and she had a white snout. The black was full black, the white a brilliant white.

Her horns were long spears, each one so close to perfectly straight they first appeared to be exactly that. Together they made a slight V from base to sharp tip, and the brass tag on the wooden trophy frame claimed they were 38 inches long.

Standing just below his trophy, Hemingway was holding forth as Papa, telling stories about the hunt and the kill while someone tracked down Brian.

"One shot from the '03 Springfield. She went down. My gun boy, a bushman, he called it a two heart beat kill."

He was surrounded by the 30 or so guests who were in camp, all of them pleased with themselves to be there.

Brian stood in the kitchen at the double doors leading to the dining hall, looking through the door's window at the crowded room; he caught his reflection in the glass and saw the blood on his face. Brian found a dishtowel and stood at the sink to clean himself up as his nuisance guest came in, smiled meekly, and continued on. The window glass to the dark outside served as a useful mirror, and after he washed his face he located the gash in his scalp with his fingers and cleaned it as best he could.

When Brian pushed through the swinging doors from the kitchen into the Great Lodge's dining hall, he reminded Hemingway of a bull entering the ring. Brian had control of his confusion but not yet his anger. He put himself to that task. He approached the crowd and the guests parted. There stood Ernest Hemingway and the moment Brian saw him, he had the urge to punch this man right in the face; he didn't know why, but his right hand tightened into a fist while he forced a smile. Then he saw that the burial shroud was a sheet, and it was lying at Hemingway's feet and Brian looked up and realized that the crate hadn't carried Maureen O'Toole but this trophy head, and he remembered that Hemingway had arrived with it to honor his wife.

Still shaking with anger, still working hard to control it, Brian stood next the writer as Hemingway turned to the purpose at hand, Papa's memorial to Maureen Burke.

"The gemsbok is unusual among the African antelope. It is the female of the species that grows the largest horns. And that's as it should be, for it's the female who uses these extraordinary horns, theses sharp spears, in deadly fashion, to protect what's hers. The muscle in her shoulders and neck provide the force behind those weapons and she is fearless with them in the face of a leopard attack, or an attack from lions, from any predator. Time and again she will drive them off. The bushmen use the tips of female gemsbok horns as the head of their spears." He puffed on his cigar. "The males, well, the males, don't misunderstand, they are outfitted with a fine set of horns themselves, just not like these. And they only use their horns to fight other males, to maintain rights to their harem, their herd of females." He puffed again, and smiled. "And I for one will never fault them for that."

The guests laughed.

Brian didn't feel like laughing.

He fully recalled what the evening was about now—the writer brought the trophy head to Innish Cove in honor of Maureen Burke. And as he became clearer about the evening, he realized he was the one person in the room who knew that Maureen O'Toole was not honorable.

Papa Hemingway continued. "As you get older it's harder to have heroes, but it is just as necessary. I didn't know Maureen as well as some of you perhaps, but during the brief three or four days I spent with her last summer, with her and with you, Brian, and Joe Loon, the impact this place had on my view of the world was wonderfully restorative, and Maureen, she was at the center of it all, reminding me that the best of the human race redeems the rest of us sinners, and that is heroic in my book."

Brian wasn't well. He was woozy. He was drunk. He was very angry. And now, it seemed, everyone was looking at him, no, staring at him. A guest gestured for him to pat his brow, and when he did he found he was bleeding again. He reached for his handkerchief but Hemingway noticed.

"Are you bleeding?"

Brian had enough control to stay Big Irish.

First he spoke to Hemingway, and all was well. "I'm fine, an' all us gathered here..." Then he spoke to his guests, and a new tone grew as he went on: a Big Irish polite dismal of the landlord. "... and we thank you, don't we fella's, we thank the famous writer, the great man, ah what an honor 'tis, for he not only comes to grace us wit' his mighty presence, he shares his trophies wit' us, yea, Hemingway's trophy, the remarkable gift, as, what..." Brian turned back to the writer. "...as a remembrance?"

Hemingway didn't like Brian's new tone at all.

"If you like."

"If I like." He looked out at the guests. "If I like." The guests didn't like this either. Brian decided he didn't care. He stepped back to get a better angle up at the gemsbok and genuflected as he spoke.

"In the name of Maureen O'Toole. The tip of the spear. All in remembrance of her."

Hemingway thought he would try one more time. "Maureen O'Toole? Her maiden name?"

"Maureen O'Toole. Her first name an' her last name."

Some of the guests in the back of the pack began to retreat from this scene, breaking away from the crowd and heading to the pub or out the door to their cabins. Brian noticed and called to them.

"We do this in remembrance of her."

There was more blood on his face. More guests turned to leave.

Brian turned to Hemingway.

"When I saw you standin' there I wanted to knock you on your arse."

"Was a time I would give you a fair fight."

"I said nothin' about lookin' for a fair fight."

The guests who heard this divided into two camps; most backed away, but Hemingway's friends and Brian's longest tenured guests stepped forward in case they were needed. With his friends at hand the writer saw the opportunity to retreat, and he did. In a few minutes more the dining hall and the pub and the billiard lounge were all empty but for Brian, who had a bottle of Tullamore Dew, which he drank to the memory of Maureen O'Toole and her deadly horns.

Mary sat on the bench in front of the statue in the Chapel far longer than she wanted to that night; she knew she needed to return to the house where Little Stevie was watching over Grace, but she also had to stay. She didn't know why, but she knew she was waiting, she felt she was waiting, for something, or someone.

After a time she returned to the house, past This Man who maintained his vigil in front of the sacred birch grove, and when she got to the house she found Little Stevie asleep on the floor at the foot of the bed where Grace slept soundly.

The next morning Brian was found lying on the floor under the gemsbok by two Ojibway women who were part of the early morning kitchen crew. They roused him; it wasn't easy, but they got him to his feet. And after breakfast two groups of guests regretfully reported they had to leave earlier than planned and asked Brian to make the necessary arrangements, and the next day Hemingway's party left early as well.

The gemsbok remained.

Every day for the rest of the season Mary found a moment to slip away to the Chapel where she would sit in front of the statue and pray for the soul of her sister Maureen, Raven Hair, and where she waited for a sign.

AUTHOR'S NOTE

IT HAS BEEN WONDERFUL to see how these novels I am writing that are based on my experiences as a fishing guide with the Ojibway on the English River in Northwest Ontario and on my time in the West of Ireland have brought so many folks together.

The families who owned the fishing camps where I worked before I worked there have discovered my novels and through them have gotten acquainted with the grandchildren of the Ojibway guides who used to work for them, and with the current owners of the camp.

In Ireland, a recent research trip for the third novel of this River of Lakes trilogy will result in teams of my Duke students working for local historian entrepreneurs who have dedicated their lives to preserving the wonder of the West of Ireland.

ABOUT THE AUTHOR

CARL NORDGREN was born in Greenville, Mississippi, where his great grandmother's house was across the street from the boyhood home of author Walker Percy. Carl has worked as a fishing guide on the English River in Northwestern Ontario and on the White River in the Arkansas Ozarks, as a bartender, as a foundry man, and as an entrepreneur. He lived with his family in Ireland for a year where he researched the IRA. Carl currently teaches courses in Creativity to undergraduate students at Duke University. His first book, *The 53rd Parallel*, was an international bestseller. He graduated from Knox College and lives in Durham, North Carolina with his wife, Marie, where they have raised three daughters.

OTHER BOOKS BY CARL NORDGREN

The 53rd Parallel
(River of Lakes, Book 1)

"Dreams of disaster and redemption... author Carl Nordgren meditates on themes of immigration and environment as well as new beginnings and old ghosts."
– The State of Things, WUNC

"A most lyrical and poetically imagined novel... to be savored."
–Mallory Heart Reviews

"Lyrical and touching, *The 53rd Parallel* brings together two very different cultures, both looking to preserve a sacred way of life."
–Looking For a Good Book

Anung's Journey

An ancient Ojibway legend, as told to Carl Nordgren by Steve Fobister. Illustrated by Brita Wolf.

"This story gently proffers a message of cooperation and harmony with nature, community members, and all the world's people."
–Foreword Reviews, 5 Stars

Named Top 10 Middle Grade Novels of 2014 by *Foreword Reviews*. INDIEFAB finalist in Juvenile Fiction and Multicultural Fiction. (Results announced June 2016.)

International Book Awards Finalist

IF YOU LIKED THIS BOOK, WE SUGGEST...

The Particular Appeal of Gillian Pugsley by Susan Örnbratt

From the shores of The Great Lakes to the slums of Bombay and a tiny island in between, this historical novel takes the reader on an intimate journey to unravel a family secret that's lain hidden for generations.

"exuberantly readable... with a delicious twist at the end—recommended"

—Historical Novel Society

"Gillian's character is memorable—feisty, unexpected and a lover of language"

—Kirkus Reviews

CPSIA information can be obtained
at www.ICGtesting.com
Printed in the USA
FFOW02n2054040615
13930FF